Echo's Sister

Also by Paul Mosier

Train I Ride

Echo's Sister

PAUL MOSIER

HARPER
An Imprint of HarperCollinsPublishers

Library of Congress Cataloging-in-Publication Data

Names: Mosier, Paul, author.
Title: Echo's sister / Paul Mosier.
Description: First edition. | New York, NY : Harper, an imprint of HarperCollinsPublishers, [2018] | Summary: "Twelve-year-old Echo finds the courage to help her younger sister fight cancer, and, in the process, finds the love and support of an entire community"—Provided by publisher.
Identifiers: LCCN 2017034538 | ISBN 9780062455673 (hardcover)
Subjects: | CYAC: Sick—Fiction. | Cancer—Fiction. | Family life—New York (State)—New York—Fiction. | Friendship—Fiction. | Schools—Fiction. | Community life—New York (State)—New York—Fiction. | New York (N.Y.)—Fiction.
Classification: LCC PZ7.1.M6773 Ech 2018 | DDC [Fic]—dc23 LC record available at https://lccn.loc.gov/2017034538

Typography by Jessie Gang
18 19 20 21 22   CG/LSCH   10 9 8 7 6 5 4 3 2 1
❖
First Edition

To Harmony Sea Mosier

1

TODAY IS THE first day of school, and it's gonna be fantastic.

I think this as I sit on the toilet in the second-floor bathroom of the Village Arts Academy in New York City, looking at a page in my tiny journal with a list of things to say to all my new classmates. The carefully crafted phrases on my list are sure to make me a big hit with all these new kids.

Technically the kids aren't new. They're just new to me. I've been going to public school my whole life, but now I'm starting seventh grade at this private arts academy.

I'll make all kinds of new friends as long as I stick to the list of things to say and don't allow conversation to stray into dangerous subjects, like money. The kids at this school generally have much more money than my family does. We can barely afford to live here in Manhattan, even though my mom is a semi-famous dress designer. The other kids mostly have rich parents who work on Wall Street. They probably all get dropped off in limousines, while our plan is for Dad to walk me to school every day.

I'm not sure why everything is so expensive in the city, because the apartments are tiny and falling apart. Or at least ours is. My dad says that the correct term for expensive and tiny and falling apart is *charming*. Mom seems to agree with him. I guess our neighborhood, which is called Greenwich Village, is kind of pretty with its trees in the sidewalk planters. Before Mom and Dad had me and Echo—my little sister— it probably felt much roomier. Now there's four of us crammed into an apartment we can barely afford and which we can't afford to leave.

Seventh grade is obviously the luckiest grade, so I'm sure that the Village Arts Academy won't crumble to the ground, even though it's, like, 150 years old. At least not while I'm in seventh grade, the luckiest. And there's really nothing wrong with this school that a million dollars' worth of disinfectant couldn't fix. Particularly in the bathrooms. This is foremost in my thoughts as I sit on the toilet reviewing my list of things to say to make a good impression on my new classmates.

In addition to Don't mention money in any way, my list says Don't compliment anyone's clothes. Everyone here wears the same uniform, so obviously that would sound stupid. And if I complimented another girl's clothes that would also be complimenting my *own* clothes, which would make me sound conceited.

My list also says Don't ask where the bathroom is. That'll be perfectly easy to not do as I'm already here. I just need to remember how to get back once I leave. Sitting in the stall is a good place to collect one's thoughts and gather one's courage, as long as nobody thinks I spend too much time in here, like there's something wrong with me or something.

It's not that I'm embarrassed that I'm, like, a physical human being who has to use the bathroom. It's just that in books and cartoons and movies the characters never have to pee. So it seems weird to bring it to anyone's attention.

One of the most important items on the list is Don't introduce yourself as Laughter, which is the actual name my parents gave me. Instead I go by "El," as in the sound of the letter my name begins with. When other girls hear it they'll just think my name is Elle, which immediately makes me sound like I've stepped from the pages of a fashion magazine, even if I'm wearing exactly the same thing as every other girl in school.

But maybe it isn't good to sound like I've stepped from the pages of a fashion magazine? I turn back to an earlier entry in my tiny journal and add it to my list of things to wonder about.

Seeing Laughter on the list reminds me that I need to tell my first-period teacher that I go by my nickname before he does the roll call. I only have about three minutes before the bell rings, so I flush the toilet even though I didn't pee, so the other girls in the bathroom won't think I was just hanging out in the stall like it's a magical unicorn vortex.

Before closing my tiny journal I notice that everything listed is things *not* to say, except Hello!

That's easy enough to remember.

Hello!

I strike the exclamation point with my pencil so I don't sound too eager.

Hello.

It occurs to me I've just said "Hello" out loud twice while looking at the list, so I now must pretend to be having a telephone conversation in the stall so that the other girls in the restroom don't think I'm someone who sits on the toilet saying hello to herself, which apparently I am.

"Yeah, I'm at school, just getting ready for first hour. Uh-huh. Yeah. Okay. Really? No way! Yep. All right. Smashing. That'd be delightful. Okay. *Ciao!*"

I might have overdone it with my conversation, which is all kinds of make-believe. In my mind I was pretending to have a conversation with Maisy, my best friend from my old school and my whole life, but I haven't actually spoken to her in weeks because she was in France for most of the summer.

Also I want Maisy to think that everything is going to be great with me at my new school, and I've had a hard time feeling like I could sound convincing. I've been really worried that I won't make any friends, and I'm sure Maisy will be able to tell I'm worried if she hears my voice. My parents won't even let me take my cell phone to school because they think I'm famous for losing things.

Finally I close my tiny journal and tuck it away in my shirt pocket, then wait a half minute to give everyone in the bathroom a chance to forget what they've just heard. I stand, straighten my uniform skirt and button-up shirt, put my book bag over my shoulder, slide the lock in the stall door, and exit with an air of nonchalance.

I avoid eye contact with the six or seven other girls

chatting in front of the mirror as I wash my hands at the sink. I glance at my face in the mirror, my light brown hair and green eyes, then wipe the chocolate from the corner of my mouth 'cause it won't do to have everyone jealous that I had a chocolate doughnut for breakfast.

Then I hurry down the hall, keeping my feet close to the wooden floors so I won't sound like I'm running, though I practically am. Then inside room 211 and to the front of the class, where there's a really good-looking man standing. But I don't care that he's gorgeous because boys don't have any effect on me.

"Hello," he says.

"Hello," I say. He's got wavy dark hair and a smiley smile. He has patches on the elbows of his sport coat.

"Are you in my first-hour class?"

"Yes," I begin, then take my voice down a few notches. "And I wanted to alert you to a mistake with my name."

"Oh? What mistake is that?" He tilts his head.

I lean in closer. "The record says my name is Laughter, but it's actually El."

"Laughter?" he asks way too loudly.

I wince. "Please just call me El when you take attendance."

He smiles. "How about I just laugh and you can

wave at me from your desk?"

I try not to smile, because he needs to know how serious I am about this.

"All right, Miss El," he says. "Please take your seat, it's almost time for—"

The bell rings long and loud, interrupting him. He smiles, and I smile back, not because he's good-looking and charming but because it's what you do when someone smiles at you.

When I turn around every desk is taken except for one in the front row, which is exactly where I was hoping not to sit. It would be one thing if the last open seat was in the front row but nearest the door, but it's right in the center, like I'm the hood ornament of the class.

"That one isn't taken." It's a girl, smiling and pointing at the seat to her right. The hood ornament seat. I furrow my brow. I'm not sure whether she's smiling because she's nice or because she's mean and fully aware that it's the very worst seat in class.

I sit in the chair, which is connected to the wooden desk, and sink down as low as I can without drawing attention to myself.

Teacher-man turns his back to the class and begins writing on the blackboard, which may possibly be as old as this building. The chalk taps and squeaks.

Then he turns to the class and smiles. I see the name he has written on the board and my jaw drops. There's a low murmur from the class behind me.

"Good morning, class, and welcome to seventh-grade English. My name is Mr. Dewfuss, an unfortunate gift from my ancestors, who made lives for themselves finding things to eat in the swamps of central Europe. Generally the enunciation of my name is followed by a chorus of . . ." He pauses and glances beneath raised eyebrows directly at me. "*Laughter*. So instead I'd prefer it if you called me Mr. D."

He returns to the chalkboard and erases everything in his name except the letter *D*.

I sit up straight. This is definitely gonna be the best year ever, and—worst seat or not—seventh-grade English with Mr. D is gonna be my favorite class.

✿ ✿ ✿

The rest of English class is pretty much perfect. We're beginning with a unit on Emily Dickinson, who is maybe my favorite poet ever. Her poems are surprising, even when you've read them a million times. But I don't let anyone in class know I've already read them a million times, 'cause I'm not sure if my classmates realize how cool it is that I have.

The bell rings, the class rises with the sounds of backpacks zipping and chairs and desks dragging on the wood floors. Having been totally absorbed in the discussion, I am the last to pack my backpack, the last to leave the class. I smile at Mr. D and he smiles back as I leave the room and enter the rest of the school day.

I glide down the hall past trophy cases, which don't have figures of athletes because they don't really do sports much at this school. So if I'm gonna keep winning tennis trophies it's gonna have to be at the racquet club, where Mom and Dad signed me up at the beginning of summer. Instead this school has cases with black-and-white photographs of bow-tied teachers standing beside children of earlier generations who won academic decathlons and art scholarships, and trophies that have no balls or bats or racquets at all.

I catch a glimpse of an old photo showing my high-school-aged dad standing before a giant canvas with a big paintbrush in hand, looking smug, but I don't stop to examine it. I pretend not to notice a photo of my pretty teenage mom smiling beside a dress form featuring one of her early designs from high school. I pretend not to notice these things because I don't want to draw attention to the fact my parents went to school here, which might make it obvious they can only afford to send me here because of the discount given to legacy students. I've already seen the photos anyway, when I took the tour early in the summer, so I keep my nose pointed down the hall in the direction of my next class.

The rest of the day is almost perfect. Math is, like, a whole year behind what I was doing at public school last year, so I'll be able to skate through it.

In history class we talk about the Minoan civilization, where kids our age had to survive jumping over a bull's horns as a rite of passage. I think the teacher, Mr. Grimm, wants us to feel like we have it easy since we don't have to jump over a bull's horns to get a passing grade, and I'm pretty sure he's going to try to make it as hard as possible for us. But I sit next to a nice girl named Emy, who invites me to sit with her at café fourth hour.

Mom packed the best-ever lunch, an almond butter and blackberry jelly sandwich, tahini coleslaw, and mango slices. I eat it with Emy in the basement cafeteria, which has tall windows through which you can watch the people walking by on the sidewalk. I share my mango with Emy and remember not to stray from my list of safe topics for conversation. I can expand that list after she and I have become inseparable. And when I get home I'll call Maisy and tell her how wonderful everything is turning out to be, and how I made a great new friend, but not to worry, as Emy will never take the place of her.

In physical education I score a goal in street hockey, which we play outside on the actual tree-lined street while bright orange barricades at either end keep cars away.

In science, a dark-haired boy who would be considered cute—by girls who care about that sort of thing—keeps looking at me, which is a good thing only because it's better than *not* attracting the notice of any of them. I mean, boys can't really help themselves at this age, and being noticed by one of them means that there's probably nothing terribly wrong with me physically.

Unless of course he's looking at me because there *is* something terribly wrong with me physically. I pull out my tiny journal and find the list of things to wonder about, and add that to it. But I'm pretty sure he's looking at me because I activated his girl-crazy radar. Boys can be so clueless they often fail to notice serious imperfections. Like one ear being way higher than the other.

I guess that's kinda sweet of them.

One ear being way higher than the other is actually one of several items on the list of serious imperfections from which I suffer. This list is also found in my tiny journal, but I try not to spend too much time looking at it. It's bad for my morale.

Seventh hour is art, and the teacher is a woman named Miss Numero Uno, who actually knows my dad from way back when he painted a lot. Miss Numero Uno doesn't embarrass me too much by drawing attention to her knowing my dad. This is fortunate because she is potentially quite embarrassing, the way that artists sometimes are. She has tattoos all over her arms and black hair with frighteningly sharp bangs, and today wears jeans with paint splattered all over them so everyone will know she's legit. She has a way of looking at you like she's deciding whether you'd be a good subject to paint, which takes a little getting used to.

Also, Miss Numero Uno isn't an actual name. I'm pretty sure that's, like, an Art World name. Her real name is probably Betty Johnson or something like that. But obviously I'm completely okay with it if she wants to be called something other than the name she was given. I totally get it.

Miss Numero Uno has us do something she calls "free expression on newsprint" while she stares out the windows of the fourth floor, which is the top level of the Village Arts Academy. I draw her staring out the windows, and as I look from Miss Numero Uno to my paper and back she strikes a pose. Her profile is backlit, like the emperor Napoleon tasting victory in the painting on the cover of our history book from third hour. She just stands there holding the pose like it's perfectly normal, even though I'm the only one drawing her and everyone else seems to be avoiding looking at her. I draw her in deep gray charcoal, and it looks pretty good.

But I start to regret my choice of subject when it occurs to me that we will be turning in the newsprint for her to evaluate. Maybe she never knew how ridiculous she looks posing against the window, in which case it's probably not good to be the one to bring it to her attention. When I'm done I give the drawing a goofy smile to disguise the drama of the pose, and so she won't think I'm very good. I don't want to draw attention to myself as particularly talented, either.

When the final bell rings I already have my book bag packed and ready to go. I leave my newsprint on my table as instructed and drift out of the art room, out of the smells of clay and linseed-oil paint, and into the hall.

I feel dreamy. It's been the best first day of school ever, and it's gonna be an amazing year.

I scan the throng of students moving down the hall, down the wide stairs, down the main hall toward the front doors, but I don't see Emy. Nor do I see the boy who stared at me in science class. But I'll see them again tomorrow. Because this school is now *my* school, and these will be my classmates and friends, more and more each day.

Out the doors I go, into the warm September afternoon. Down the wide gray steps, onto the sidewalk.

My dad is standing there.

I stop cold.

"Why are you here?"

He smiles awkwardly, bounces on his heels. "Just wanted to see how your first day went."

I frown. This is not part of the plan. He wasn't supposed to meet me. I was supposed to walk home myself.

"What's wrong?" I ask.

My classmates stream past. A terrible feeling descends upon me, like the sky is falling.

"What?" I ask.

"Come on." His arms reach out to me, ready for an embrace.

2

DAD STEERS ME into a fast-food Indian place a half block from school. While he's at the counter ordering for us, I sit at the greasy linoleum table reviewing a list in my tiny journal of bad news I'm expecting to eventually hear. Because I'm more than pretty sure I'm about to hear something along those lines.

I'm a big fan of using my tiny journal to make lists. My dad says that they are my unique attempt at imposing order on a chaotic universe. By that he means I'm trying to make a crazy world less crazy. When he says *universe*, he holds out his hands like he's putting the word in quotation marks, because when he says *chaotic universe* he's talking about my brain.

At the top of the list is *Mom and Dad are getting a divorce,* though I should probably move that down the list. They haven't been stressed out lately, and I haven't had any friends whose parents are getting a divorce in a while. Not that other kids' parents divorcing should make me worry that mine will, but that's how it seems to work in my head.

Also on the list are things like *Meowzers has squandered his ninth and final life* or *Grandma has passed into the next dimension*. Meowzers and Grandma are both really old, so either of those could happen any time. One of the things that *was* on the list was *Grandpa has kicked the bucket*, but it's crossed off because it actually happened. There are some things you can worry about that can happen more than once, but a particular person kicking the bucket is not one of them.

That was incredibly sad, Grandpa dying, and it proved to me that things you worry about sometimes do happen.

I slip the journal back into my front pocket as Dad comes to join me at the table. As we wait for the garlic naan to arrive, I sip water and worry about which one of the things on the list of bad news I'm expecting to hear is going to be sprung on me.

"This place has been here since my school days," Dad says. "It's where I stole your mom's heart, between bites of vegetable korma."

I smile, but I can't picture the scene. I'm too preoccupied.

"So, how was your first day?" he asks.

"Fine. What did you bring me here to tell me?" I just kinda blurt it out.

Dad takes a sip of water, noisily slurping from his glass. I look at him and smile, then raise my glass and do the same. Every now and then we do this for fun. We're always talking about how we'll go to an ice-cream place or restaurant but only order water and then sit there and do this obnoxious slurping.

Having lightened the mood, he's now ready to give me some kind of bad news. He pushes his water away and begins.

"Remember last week when we took Echo to the orthodontist?"

"Yes, I remember." I feel relief. He's probably gonna tell me she'll need braces. I already have braces, and they're really expensive. Hopefully it won't cut into next summer's vacation funds too much.

"We saw her front teeth were starting to stick out. And get crooked."

"I know," I say.

One of the restaurant's employees—an Indian man in a long shirt—comes out with the naan. He recognizes Dad and lights up.

"Tate! It's good to see you. This beautiful young woman must have gotten her good looks from Grace, yes?"

"Ha! It's good to see you, Hari. This is El, our older daughter. El, this is Hari."

"Nice to meet you," I say.

Hari smiles and does a little bow. "Nice to see you again, El. I remember when you were just a babe in your parents' arms. But it's been too long! And I hope we see more of you."

Dad gestures to me. "I'm sure she'll be a regular, just like her mom and dad."

Before withdrawing he sets the naan down in front of us. It smells heavenly.

Dad clears his throat. "So, back to Echo's front teeth sticking out. The orthodontist seemed like the right place to take her for that."

I nod, tearing a bite-size strip from the Indian bread.

"But the orthodontist sent us to an oral surgeon."

"Oh?" I say through a delicious mouthful.

"And she sent us to an ear, nose, and throat specialist, which is where we took Echo this morning."

"If they're specialists, shouldn't they pick one of the three? 'Ear, nose, and throat' sounds like Neapolitan ice cream, which is exactly what you pick when you can't decide."

He doesn't smile. "And then the ENT sent us to the ER."

"The what?"

"The emergency room."

"For an overbite?" I'm about to take another bite of naan, but I set it down on the plate. "Why?"

Dad clears his throat. "Her teeth were being pushed forward by something growing in her mouth."

"What do you mean, *something*?"

"A tumor."

"A *tumor*?"

"Yes." He tears off a piece of naan and stuffs it into his mouth. I can tell he's trying to play it down, like you can just say *tumor* and then enjoy a bite of naan. "So she's been admitted to the hospital."

"Why?"

He swallows and washes it down with a sip of water. "To do tests. There are all sorts of tumors. So, they just want to figure out what it is and then decide what they want to do with it."

I watch him tear off another bite. He watches me back.

"Don't worry." He smiles a totally fake smile. "Everything is gonna be all right."

I nod.

There's no way I'm adding this, or any future possible consequences of this, to my list of bad news I'm waiting to hear. Echo is only six. She can sometimes be annoying, but when I think about it, she is pretty much the best little sister I could hope for. I'm not even going to think about what kinds of bad news I might wait for, because it isn't gonna be anything like that. Echo is gonna be fine.

She's only six.

❀ ❀ ❀

"So, tell me about your first day at school."

I think Dad asks me about school again on the walk home because he doesn't want me asking about Echo any more. But I suppose he'd ask about school anyway, especially on the first day.

"It was good." It had been *great*, but I'm downgrading it.

"Did you make any new friends?"

"Tons." Maybe one, really, but he'd rather hear tons.

"How was art class?"

"Fine. Miss Numero Uno is beyond strange. She's always striking poses. She strikes poses between the instructions she gives. And she strikes *long* poses while we work. Like *this*." I stop on the sidewalk and bend my body, twist my neck, put the back of my hand against my forehead.

He chuckles. "Same old Miss Numero Uno."

"How do you know her, again?"

He kicks a pebble down the sidewalk. "I used to know her from the art world. She's a painter, I was a painter."

"You're *still* a painter."

He shrugs. "If you say so. But I'm not painting at the moment."

"Does she know I'm your daughter? I felt like she was looking at me funny. Like she was deciding whether she wanted to paint me."

"Well, she *is* a painter. I haven't been in contact with her. She might have guessed by your last name." He spots another pebble ahead and stutters his steps to line up another kick. "And because you look like your mother, whom she also knew. It's also possible that you'd feel like she was looking at you funny without my having known her."

I turn to him. "Because I'm the sort of girl who thinks people are looking at me funny?"

He smiles and starts up the front steps of our brownstone apartment. "Maybe because she's inclined to give people funny looks."

He punches the code into the keypad and I push the door open. We head up the two flights of stairs to our two-bedroom apartment. "Miss Numero Uno is known in the art world for her eccentricity," he says. "The school puts up with a lot of strangeness from her because it looks good to have her as part of the art staff." We arrive at our door, one of two on the third floor. He pulls the key from his pocket and unlocks it.

We are met by the white and green light of our living room. It's white from the walls and green from the tree filling the window, growing up from the sidewalk planter outside.

My list of attractive features of our apartment, somewhere near the beginning of my current tiny journal, goes something like this:

One: Almost located in the Village. (Practically. I was barely exaggerating when I said we lived in Greenwich Village.)

Two: Tree-lined street. (Also lined with parked cars on both sides.)

Three: Almost never find people sleeping at the top of the steps outside, because there isn't much of a landing.

Four: Small size encourages close-knit family.

Five: Small size makes for quick cleaning.

Six: Small size means everything is within reach at all times.

Seven: Neighborhood is colorful and interesting. And not just the negative sort of colorful and interesting.

The apartment really is kinda pretty in spite of being tiny and ancient and falling apart, but at the moment it's mostly too quiet. Echo is conspicuously absent.

Outside they're tearing up the street with scraping machines and the town house next door is being gutted so that rich people can make it fabulous and then move in, so there's plenty of noise. But there's no Echo talking to herself while she plays. There isn't the sound of her practicing the keyboard while forgetting to use the headphones so we get to hear the same twenty notes of music over and over again. Nor is she reading aloud like she does, which always drives me crazy. I've been so looking forward to the day she will read silently. But I wouldn't mind hearing it right now.

Echo and I share a room, which is the quietest of all at this moment. I should just enjoy having it to myself, 'cause soon enough it'll get crowded and noisy again. But, to be honest, it's making me sad.

I remember when Echo was born and she came home from the hospital. At first she was in Mom and Dad's room, but before she turned one, when she could sleep through the night, she moved into my room. First in a crib, and then Dad put together a bunk bed for us to share. I didn't think I'd like sharing a room with her, but I kinda got used to her and the little noises she makes in her sleep, babbling and then talking to herself as she got older. She's always sort of hid behind me whenever we're in public. So naturally she'd be happy to have me near enough to be in my shadow, even when we sleep. And she *does* sleep right beneath me, in the lower bunk of our bunk bed.

Mom and Dad say it's perfectly normal, but everything I do, she wants to do. If I draw a unicorn, she draws a unicorn. She doesn't have any original ideas, and I think Mom and Dad ought to encourage her to do her own thing instead of mimicking me. But right now I wouldn't mind having her around, doing exactly whatever I'm doing. And if she *was* around I wouldn't be doing what I *am* doing, which is standing in the middle of the room feeling sad.

I turn on the radio to quiet the emptiness. My dad has glued the dial so it's stuck on the public radio classical station. He thinks it's going to make me and Echo grow up to be geniuses or something, but I've kind of gotten used to it by now. I actually like it, though I didn't talk about liking it with any of the kids at my old school, except the ones in band.

I climb into my bed and open my English textbook to the Emily Dickinson section. It includes only five of her poems, which isn't nearly enough, and it doesn't include any of my favorites. But that's okay.

I begin reading one of them. It's about a fly buzzing on a window in a room where everyone is waiting for the narrator to die.

I read it, and I look to the window expecting to see a fly. There isn't one, but the room seems suddenly darker.

I slam the book shut.

I can read Emily Dickinson later.

Dad picks up Chinese food for the two of us for dinner, since Mom is still at the hospital with Echo. Sometimes it's fun when it's just Dad and me for dinner—eating takeout at the table—but it doesn't feel fun tonight. I put on the classical station to try to brighten things, but they're playing some gloomy nineteenth-century funeral march.

Opening fortune cookies is always fun, so I crack mine open before I'm even done eating to try to change the mood.

"What's it say?" Dad asks.

I unfold it, then turn it over. It's blank on both sides.

"This can't be good." I show it to Dad.

"No news is good news." He's always trying to see the bright side of things.

"*Good* news is good news," I say, correcting him. "Can I have yours?"

"Sure." He slides his cookie across the table to me. I crack it open, but his fortune says *Having a party? Ask about our catering!*

That's the worst—when your fortune cookie tries to sell you something or impart some ancient wisdom instead of telling you what to expect. Really what I'd hoped is that it would say *Echo is going to be fine.* But no fortune cookie ever said that.

After dinner I do the dishes and we head out to the hospital. It's a pretty evening, the late summer light draining from the sky over the apartments and town houses, but it doesn't seem right. I know the neighborhood perfectly well, but walking to the subway station it seems different. The trees smell like trees, the bodega smells like bodega, but everything is just a little bit off.

On the subway I make a list of things that are possibly wrong with Echo. Dad is used to seeing me with a pencil in one hand and my tiny journal in the other, and if I don't offer to show him what I'm working on, he doesn't ask to see. As the subway rolls uptown I come up with these:

Possible Diagnoses for Echo
Thorn in Paw
Ice-Cream Allergy
Hoof and Mouth Disease
Scrivener's Palsy (Writer's Cramp)
Stink Eye
Abdominal Abomination
Crazy Face

It's a good list but it doesn't work. It doesn't make me smile and it doesn't distract me.

Dad reaches for my hand as we walk down the side-walk on the few blocks between the subway and the hospital.

"I love my first-period teacher," I say. "Mr. D." I'm saying this to change the subject in my head from how much I hate hospitals, how scared I am of them.

"What does he teach?"

"English." I'm not thinking of the time Grandpa went to the hospital and died.

"English is always your favorite."

"Yeah. But I can tell Mr. D is gonna be especially

27

great. We're already reading Emily Dickinson." I'm not thinking about the moaning in the corridors or the assorted unpleasant smells, like mop buckets that the cleaning crews roll around to soak up everything dreadful that's supposed to be inside someone's body that somehow ends up on the floor. I'm not thinking about how every time I walk into a hospital every part of my body that has ever hurt starts hurting again.

We walk through the entrance, and in spite of the colorful paintings of zoo animals on the walls meant to make the sick children happy, my arm hurts from memories of vaccinations. We stand at the reception desk and I feel my wrist broken from falling off my skateboard three years ago. Walking to the elevators my toe aches from when I broke it on the dresser leg last year. The elevator door opens on the seventh floor and I feel every headache I've ever had, all piled up as one.

We step off. Having been here earlier today, Dad knows the way to Echo's room.

"Remember, honey—stay positive."

"Why *wouldn't* I be positive?"

"Exactly. Everything's going to be fine. But be super nice."

"Why *wouldn't* I be?"

He smiles. "Do you feel okay?"

"Of course." I start to feel dizzy.

The young nurse at the desk stands up. She's wearing polar bear scrubs that look like pajamas. "Are you breathing, sweetheart?"

"Why wouldn't I be breathing?" Because, as I realize, I've just forgotten to. So I take a big gulp of air as Dad grabs my arm to steady me.

The nurse comes to my side. "Nice deep breaths. In through your nose, then out through your mouth. Nice and slow."

I nod.

"You okay?" the nurse asks.

I nod again.

"Are you Echo's sister?"

"Yes."

She smiles. "She looks like a miniature version of you. She's very spirited."

My mouth smiles, and Dad holds my hand as we walk down the hall.

Everyone always says that. That she's my mini-me. She was named Echo because she looked just like I did when I was born, and my dad started laughing and crying simultaneously and uncontrollably exactly the way he did when he saw *me* being born. I was the Laughter; she was the Echo.

I think she got the better end of *that* deal.

We enter room 726 and move inside.

"Hello!" we say.

"Hi!" Echo looks happy.

"Hello, El," Mom says. "Please wash your hands before you go near Echo. We need to get in the habit of doing that. Okay, honey?"

I nod and join Dad, who is already at the sink lathering his hands. Echo is in a big bed with wheels and metal rails on the sides, the kind that keep you from falling out. She's hooked up to an IV that's dripping some sort of clear liquid into her arm. She's wearing a blue gown with dolphins and sailboats all over it. A Disney movie plays on a TV up high on the wall opposite her bed. All of it makes me feel sick, and mad, like they're trying to trick Echo into thinking this is a happy place.

Dad stands beside her bed. "How you feeling, kiddo?"

"Good." She says it like she means it. Like she doesn't have a care in the world, like this is a vacation spot and not a place people come to have body parts removed.

I look to Mom, who's smiling, but it's kind of a grim smile. She's as pretty and elegant as ever, with her freckles and sharply cut brown hair, but there's a

30

shadow of worry across her face.

Down the hall a baby cries.

"They're bringing me a Popsicle!" Echo says.

"Lucky." I move to the bench by the window and sit. I remember to breathe. A big breath in, then hold it, and let it out. Echo is going to be okay.

A kid on a bed is rolled past our door. He's breathing through a tube.

"They have movies all the time," Echo says. Dad turns to the TV to see what she's watching. They're both smiling.

A sound at the window spins my head around. It's a big fly, bumping up against the glass, trying to get out of here. Like the Emily Dickinson poem, where the people are gathered waiting for someone to die.

It knocks me from the bench.

"El?" Mom rises from her chair. "What happened?"

I'm on the floor, trying to rise from the cold tiles with my palms. "I heard a fly buzz."

Then I get dizzier, and everything goes black.

When I come around I've been lifted onto the cushiony bench by the window. Mom and Dad and a nurse are hovering over me.

"How do you feel?" The nurse has two fingers

against my wrist, checking my pulse.

"Fine." The fly buzzes at the window, and I lift my head to look at him.

Mom is sitting behind my head. "She's a little bit famous for not enjoying being in hospitals." She smooths my hair out of my face.

"Have you eaten today?" the nurse asks.

I nod. "For lunch I had an almond butter and black-berry jelly sandwich. And mango slices. And tahini coleslaw."

"Who's packing *your* lunch?" the nurse asks. "I want them to pack mine, too." She lets go of my wrist.

"And we stopped at an Indian place for naan after school." Dad loves talking about Indian food. He always mentions it when we've eaten it.

"And we had dinner before we came," I say. "Chinese." I try to remember my fortune cookie fortune but I can't.

"No health problems?" The nurse is looking at my mom. I tilt my head back and see Mom shake hers.

I sit up. "Can we go now?"

Dad looks to Mom. "Well," he begins, "let's visit with Echo for a while."

I look across the room at Echo. She's holding a cherry Popsicle, watching the movie. Something on-screen makes her laugh.

"She's staying?"

Mom puts her hand back on my hair. "They want to do more tests."

"Why?"

"Just to make sure everything is okay."

"Didn't you just tell the nurse Echo doesn't have any health problems?"

Mom smiles faintly. "We were talking about *you.*"

3

WEDNESDAY I WAKE to the sound of jackhammers in the street and an electric saw in the town house next door. They wait until seven o'clock, and then it gets very loud very suddenly, like midnight on New Year's Eve, but not as much fun. It didn't bother me so much yesterday, 'cause I was practically awake all night with excitement about my first day at a new school. This morning, I'm filled with worry. The first thing to enter my mind is that Echo is waking up in the hospital. Her bed beneath me is still, the breakfast table will be too quiet. We won't be fighting over the orange juice, but I wish we would be.

I shouldn't worry. She's six years old. Terrible things don't happen to kids that young.

Practically never.

Even so, the thought of getting through day two at my new school seems overwhelming.

My phone buzzes on the dresser, and I cross the room to look at the screen. It's a message from Maisy.

Good morning! How do you like your new school? PS 022 isn't the same without you!

I don't want to get into it right now, because I don't want to tell the truth and I'm terrible at lying, just like my dad. You can tell I'm lying even on a text message.

Maisy is so together and so perfect, with the best vacations and the best everythings. I don't want to talk about the hospital because I'm sure I won't be able to sound like I'm not terrified of what might happen to Echo, even though I keep telling myself everything will be okay. So I just send emojis of a thumbs-up and of a girl running, like I'm in too much of a hurry to text right now.

I brush my teeth in the hall bathroom, which in this apartment is the *only* bathroom. Fortunately having only one bathroom is *charming*, as my dad frequently reminds me. He always reminds me that some of the hotels in the neighborhood have bathrooms that you have to share with other guests, which is supposed to make me happy I only have to share ours with three other family members. And Meowzers, whose litter box is beside the toilet. But today I only have to share it with Meowzers and Dad.

Brush-brush-brush. I spit the minty foam into the sink and give a big smile to my reflection.

"Hi! My name is El, and my little sister is in the hospital! But she'll be fine!"

It's a serious dent in my armor. With all the worries that come with being at a new school, I can't afford to be distracted and vulnerable.

I put my toothbrush away and walk into the kitchen, where Dad is sitting at the table.

"Good morning," he says.

"Good morning! My name is El, and my sister is in the hospital! But she'll be fine!"

Dad furrows his brow and raises his coffee for a sip. "I'm sure she will, honey."

There are two formerly frozen waffles on a plate at my table setting. They aren't quite fully toasted by the looks of them, so I smile at Dad and without a word return them to the toaster.

I pour myself a hot tea, which generally helps me wake up, though I have my doubts it will work today.

I get the grass-fed butter from the fridge and set it on the table since Dad forgot to, then sit down.

I stir a healthy amount of sugar into my tea, by

which I mean an amount that might be considered unhealthy. Then I take a sip.

The toaster announces toasted waffles, and I spring from my chair to get them. I carry them hot—*ow*—bare-handed to the table and drop them on my plate.

But while I'm buttering the waffles and drizzling them with syrup, and eating them bite by bite, the thought of Echo in the hospital creeps back into my mind. The thought grows larger and larger—the picture of Echo waking up in a hospital bed, with a bag of clear liquid dripping into her arm for breakfast—and it crowds out every other thought and sensation. The sweet butter and maple fades from my mouth until I can't taste it at all, and I look down at my empty plate and wonder where it went.

Dad walks me to school. It's a beautiful morning, but it somehow feels fake, or like it's conspiring against us. It's not a *real* beautiful morning, it's the facade of a beautiful morning with fear lurking behind it, like a movie where everything looks fine but you know that it's about to get very bad.

But it's not going to get very bad. Echo is just a little girl.

In English with Mr. D, I feel like I'm listening to class from the bottom of a swimming pool. I can hear talking but it doesn't really get through.

"El, do you have a response to any of the poems?" He stands before my desk, bouncing on his heels. I have a sinking feeling that he called on me twice but I didn't answer the first time. "Was there one that had a strong impact on you?"

I wonder how he possibly knew. How he read my mind.

"You seemed excited to begin the Emily Dickinson unit," he says. "Do you have a favorite?"

"Not a favorite," I say, looking at the button pinned to his coat, which features an image of a very prim Emily Dickinson. "'I heard a Fly buzz' made me dizzy."

A few kids laugh. I can't believe that slipped out of my mouth.

"Dizzy?" Mr. D folds his hands together under his chin in a thinking pose. "That's an interesting response."

"Breaths held." My words escape. "Buzzing. And then . . ."

He waits, watching me. I glance at the girl who sits to my left. She's looking at me with big eyes, like maybe I'm crazy. Mr. D keeps waiting.

I take a deep breath, because I've forgotten to breathe again.

"Yes," Mr. D finally says, breaking the spell. "It's a powerful poem. How did Emily Dickinson get into the space of the fly, and the witnesses, and the dying narrator?"

Silence from my classmates.

"Thank you, El." He smiles at me. I smile back. But exchanging smiles about a poem that made the hospital even more terrifying than usual seems like a strange thing to be doing.

The rest of the school day is even worse.

In math, I somehow missed that there was a second side to the homework page, so even though I got practically 100 percent on the first side, I got zero on the back.

In history, I'm happy to be sitting next to Emy again. But then at the very beginning of class a woman who's apparently her mom bursts through the door to tell her she's been accepted to the Midtown Academy of Ancient Music, which evidently was her first choice, and which she was on a wait list for. So she screams with happiness right in the middle of class and then gets up and leaves forever, without even looking over her shoulder at me. So I sit in my seat in shock, which quickly turns to despair, as instead of being with Emy I'm stuck with a boy named Charles to make a diorama illustrating some part of Minoan civilization. And though he looks like he's in a hurry to be an adult in a blue sport coat and his hair combed with hair oil, he smells like he's never taken a shower.

Several times while we sit together brainstorming and discussing who will do what on our assignment, I catch a Charles-scented breeze and feel like I'm gonna throw up. As a result I take about half as many breaths as I might ordinarily take during an hour-long class, and so I feel dizzy and have a headache by the time the bell rings.

Dad forgot to make my lunch, and *I* forgot to make my lunch, and I forgot to ask about what I'm supposed to eat, so not only do I not have anyone to sit with since Emy has ditched this school, I've also got no food. Fortunately there's just enough change in the bottom of my backpack to get a chocolate milk from the old ladies with the hairnets who dish out the grub. I've fabricated a story in my head that I'm on antibiotics for swamp fever and can't have anything but chocolate milk just in case the hairnets or anyone else asks, but nobody does. And while I sit alone in the cafeteria, I keep looking at the clock on the wall to make anyone who might be looking at me think that I've got somewhere important to be or something. And I *do* wish I had somewhere to be, somewhere away from this school and this worry.

In phys ed we play street hockey again, and I score

another goal, but this time I score it in the wrong net because I'm distracted and somehow lose track of which goal is which. Since this is extremely embarrassing, I pretend that I did it on purpose, and try to high-five the other team, but everyone ends up getting annoyed and thinking I'm weird. All around me the other students have friends or seem to be making friends, but I'm feeling like a combination of invisible and laughable.

In science with Mr. Bleeker we do a unit called "Why Seventh Graders Are Foul-Smelling. A Scientific Investigation." It sounds like it should be fun, or that at least it will teach me why Charles smells like he's rotting from within, but it *isn't* fun because it's so obvious Bleeker doesn't like kids. I start to worry that maybe *I* stink as bad as Charles, and try to remember when I last took a shower as Bleeker discusses the various anatomical and developmental reasons seventh graders suddenly need to step it up with the bathing and deodorants. Worse, the cute boy who kept looking at me yesterday—whose name I learned is Octavius—keeps looking at me today, but now I think it's definitely because there's something wrong with me.

I've been looking forward to seventh-hour art class all day. I'm hoping I can get lost in whatever the assignment is, and stop thinking and worrying about Echo for a while.

Unfortunately, instead of an assignment Miss Numero Uno shows a video called *The Proper Care of Art Materials*. She greets us at the door with a frown drawn on her mouth and eyebrows with charcoal to demonstrate how unhappy she is at how we handled the classroom supplies the previous day. So instead of losing myself in an art assignment, we have to watch a video so dull it allows my thoughts to drift constantly to Echo. By the end of it I'm pretty sure I still have no idea how to clean brushes after painting with oils, and my stomach aches from worrying about my sister.

After school, after the walk home and Mediterranean takeout for dinner, Dad and I are back down in the subway station waiting for the train to take us to Midtown.

There's a skinny, youngish guy with a scruffy beard playing a piano on the platform between the uptown tracks and the downtown tracks. I'm amazed that he's brought the piano down here on a big six-wheel dolly, which stands beside it. And while it isn't a *big* piano, it's a piano. He plays it well, an old jazz song. Old jazz songs were exactly what I played when we had a real piano and I had lessons twice every week. But as Echo and I have gotten bigger our apartment has seemed smaller, so Mom and Dad sold the piano and traded it for a keyboard, which is almost always folded up and stowed away in the closet. Hearing this guy play brings back the happy memory of our old piano.

"Can we give him a dollar?" I ask.

Dad looks at the piano guy. He watches, listens for a moment. "Nah, we need to save our money."

"Just a dollar? He brought his whole piano down here."

Dad turns to me. "So if he was playing something small like a ukulele or a harmonica you wouldn't want to tip him?"

"He plays really well," I say, furrowing my brow. "But the difficulty of bringing the piano helps his case."

"What if he just brought something really heavy down the stairs, like a bookcase? He could put a sign out that said 'Hey, man, how about a dollar? I just dragged this heavy bookcase down here.'"

I frown. "If you don't want to tip him, we should cover our ears."

Dad smiles. I can never make him stop smiling. Finally he reaches for his wallet and hands me a five.

I return Dad's smile and curtsy. I'm not sure why. Then I take the five and bring it to the man and his jar on the piano. He's got lots of paper money in there. He smiles and nods at me as I put it in.

It feels good to do it, even though it was Dad's money. Right now I'm so glad the man on the piano is down here making the subway station a more cheerful place. And maybe it makes New York City feel just a little bit magical or miraculous—that a skinny, scruffy guy has brought a piano down into the subway, like a little ant with a giant crumb on his back.

Then our train comes screeching in, momentarily drowning out the notes. We step on, the doors close, and we leave behind the magic and the music and enter the dark tunnel beneath the city.

At the hospital, Dad and I walk into the open door of Echo's room.

"El! Daddy!" Echo opens her arms for hugs.

"Hands, please," Mom says. "There's lots of sickness going around."

Dad and I take turns washing our hands at the sink, then take turns hugging Echo.

"El, watch this! It's funny!" Echo is watching a cartoon. I sit on the edge of her bed.

Mom and Dad begin speaking in hushed tones across the room.

"Look at this guy!" Echo says, tugging my arm. "He flies with his beard!"

I watch, but I'm having a hard time getting into it. I'm distracted by trying to hear what Mom and Dad are talking about, and it's just weird to even think of trying to laugh at something in this place.

There's a dry-erase board on the wall where ten faces with expressions ranging from ecstatic to miserable measure the amount of pain Echo is reporting, but none of them are circled. The board also says which nurses are on duty tonight.

I catch a snippet of conversation from Mom. "She's not being very understanding."

Echo laughs. I look to the screen but my ear is tuned in to Mom. I wonder if she's talking about Echo or me.

"Bring my bag tomorrow and at least I can get some sketching done." Mom glances toward me and Echo, and I look back to the screen. "It's not my fault this happened right before Fashion Week."

She must be talking about her boss, who's always pressuring her. Since Mom is a dress designer, this is a crazy time of year for her, getting new designs ready for Fashion Week. All over Manhattan the city is ramping up for it, with a huge tent set up at Bryant Park, where models on runways will display what's coming next in clothing. The sidewalks of Midtown are crowded with models eating frozen yogurt behind their designer sunglasses, carrying their portfolios under their arms.

Dad clears his throat. "Well, tomorrow we'll have a better idea."

I look from the screen to Echo, who's got a mostly finished food tray in front of her. She's had veggie stir-fry and ice cream and apple juice.

"The food looks good," I say.

"I stuffed myself," Echo says. "I don't get to eat after midnight because they're taking pictures of me in the morning."

"Don't forget to say 'cheese.'"

She makes a crazy face. "Not those kind of pictures, El!"

"I'm just kidding," I say. But my ear is still tuned to the other side of the room, where Mom and Dad continue their quiet conversation.

"It's not like I can have my dress forms set up in here," Mom says. "Does she expect me to turn this place into a dress shop?"

I listen for more, but all I hear is silence and gloom from that side of the room.

Meanwhile, Echo seems really happy. It's like she's on vacation. We don't have TV at home, so she thinks it's like when we're staying in a hotel. She doesn't have to go to school and worry about making friends among a pack of strangers, or crazy new teachers. Instead of beginning first grade she gets to watch cartoons and kid movies all day, and go to the play area, and make crafts. Mom told Dad that Echo is getting bored but it sounds like a pretty good trade-off to me.

But her tumor seems like it's bigger. Looking at her in profile, her teeth are sticking way out, which doesn't look good. Straight on she still looks cute even though her front teeth are now really crooked, but from the side she looks transformed.

And her tumor is growing. I can practically hear it.

4

THURSDAY. IT'S ECHO'S third day in the hospital and nobody knows anything yet. Or maybe they know but they're just not telling me.

I'm so tired from the hospital visits in the evening and homework late into the night, the first hours of school are a blur. I doze off in each of the first three classes. That's never happened to me before. Not until phys ed after lunch do I feel awake.

In science I get paired with the cute boy. We're supposed to identify different kinds of rocks by looking at them and touching them and banging on them and pouring liquids onto them, seeing how they react. The cute boy goes to fetch the tray of rocks and stuff, because I'm apparently in too much of a fog to be of any use.

He pushes his desk over until it bumps against mine. I look down at the rocks in the tray, then up at his face. I want to push his wavy dark hair out of his eyes. Thankfully he does it for me.

"Hey," he says.

"Hey," I say.

"My name is Octavius."

I already knew his name, which kind of stands out during roll call. "Nice to meet you, Octavius."

"Nice to meet you, Elle."

I feel myself blush. Maybe because I'm possibly allergic to rocks, and maybe because he knew my name and because it feels like he spelled my name E-L-L-E when he said it. Even though it doesn't make any sense to feel that he spelled it a certain way when he spoke it.

He reaches into the tray, which is in fact a cardboard shoebox that says *The Wanderer, size 9.* I wonder whether Mr. Bleeker is wearing a pair of The Wanderer in size nine.

Octavius holds up a pinkish rock, which has a tiny sticker with the number 1 on it.

"This is feldspar," he says. "We can skip the testing on it." He writes *feldspar* on the sheet next to the number one.

"How do you know it's feldspar?"

He looks into my eyes. "If I tell you you'll think I'm very uncool."

"Maybe I *already* think you're uncool." It's not like me to say something like that. Fortunately he smiles.

"It's a dreadful story. I had a great-uncle who was a rock enthusiast, and he made me learn all about this stuff. When he walked he used to drag his left leg behind him, because he hurt it falling down a mine shaft."

"Really?"

He smiles. "No. But that story is better than the truth. The real story is that I got a tray of rocks for my twelfth birthday."

I smile. Not a real smile, but the shape of a smile at least. "How lucky for me to be paired with you." He keeps staring into my eyes. I clear my throat. "Because you know so much about rocks." I look down into the tray and touch one of the stones.

"Right," he says. "I'm a gem of a boy."

I touch another rock, one that's flat and smooth, dark gray with white stripes. Finally I look up.

"Is that supposed to be a joke?"

He raises his eyebrows. "What?"

"Exactly. It wasn't funny." I pick up the one labeled with the number 2 sticker. "So what's this?"

"I don't know that one. Taste it."

"Really?"

He looks at the instructions. "Number two." He nods. "Yep."

I touch it to the tip of my tongue. It tastes like rock.

"You just tasted number two," he observes.

I furrow my eyebrows. "Is *that* supposed to be funny?"

"Again, no. It's just an observation."

I smile. But again, it's not really a smile. Just the shape. I put the rock back in the tray.

"It's jasper," he says.

I look at him. "You're sure?"

"Sadly, yes." He writes it on the sheet.

"Was I really supposed to taste it?"

"Yes, but I already knew it was jasper."

"Sadly." I reach for rock number three. "How about this?"

He leans back in his chair. "So far I've been doing all the work."

I smirk, but I don't really mean it. It's just the shape of a smirk. "It isn't work if you already know the answer."

He leans forward. He puts his hand on my wrist, on

my visitor bracelet from the hospital.

"What's this?"

"It's a bracelet." I pull my arm away.

I should have taken it off. When you take it off you have to get a new one on your next visit. But keeping it on gives me away as someone who has to spend every free moment visiting a loved one in the hospital instead of doing normal kid things.

"Where did you get it? I'd like to get one for my girlfriend."

I sit on my hand, the one with the bracelet on my wrist. "That's not a real question. Do I have to do the tests on rock number three? Or are you gonna amaze me with your rock knowledge?"

He smirks. "That's funny. Sad, but funny. Who's in the hospital?"

"My grandma. But it's none of your business." I really mean this. I look at rock number three and turn it over in my hand. I pretend to be interested in it.

"Every day a hospital bracelet." He takes the rock from my hand, then puts it back in the tray and writes *agate* on line number three. "Every day the tired eyes. The spacey stare."

"What's your point?"

"I recognized the bracelets right away," he says.

"Midtown Children's Hospital."

My brow furrows.

"My mom's a doctor," he adds quickly. "So . . ." He looks at rock number four. "The cafeteria is pretty solid, huh?"

Now he's trying to be all cozy with me, like he can relate. "I have to go to the bathroom," I say. "Sorry."

I leave the classroom quickly. I don't want to know what kind of doctor his mom is or how he's familiar with the cafeteria at Midtown Children's Hospital. I don't want to know his story, and I sure don't want to talk about mine.

I hurry down the hall to the bathroom. I've spent way too much time in the bathroom this first week of school, staring at the door of the stall in front of me.

I sit on the toilet and pull my tiny journal from my shirt pocket. I turn to a list I began last night.

Plausible Reasons Why I Am Not Myself

Afraid I won't make any friends at my new school.
Town house next door is being noisily gentrified.
My apartment is haunted.

Then I take my little pencil from behind my ear and add the words

Little sister has a disease that might possibly kill her.

I look at the line I've just written, then shake my head and cross it out. Then I stare at the floor. "Echo is going to be fine." As I speak to the tile floor, the words echo and come back to me. I hear my words but I'm not sure I believe them.

I close my tiny journal and slide it back into my shirt pocket. Then I flush the toilet. I don't know why, because I didn't pee and nobody is even in here. Then I wash my hands and head back down the hall to class. Before going back in, I pause with my hand on the doorknob. I make up my mind that, cute or not, Octavius doesn't get to see me suffering over Echo. And he doesn't get to know about *her* suffering. Even though Echo doesn't seem to have any idea that she *is* suffering.

Miss Numero Uno's eyebrows are natural in seventh hour. There's no charcoal to show us how disappointed she is with us, and she seems subdued. It might be my imagination, but it's almost like she feels remorse for being ridiculous the day before. She really should.

At every table there is a small mirror on a stand, like a makeup mirror, but more old-fashioned looking. We take our seats as Miss Numero Uno stares out the window. She poses dramatically against the wall of windows, where the cloudy sky presents her, backlit in a posture of sadness. She delivers the assignment without looking at the class.

"On your desk are a mirror, a sheet of newsprint, and a Conté crayon." She says it without emotion, as if she is exhausted. "You will look in the mirror. You will draw what you see. Then you will leave your work on the table and exit the class in an orderly fashion."

I look toward the windows. The light from the clouds is white, but when I stare into it, I can see the gray of the stone building across the street, and the green of the trees that reach this high. I don't know if I've ever noticed this about light.

I turn to the mirror and see myself. I look as exhausted as Miss Numero Uno sounded in delivering the assignment. I don't want to look at myself or draw myself. So I tilt the mirror until it shows a portion of the ceiling. It's covered in white decorative tin, with a water stain of brown. This is what I draw. First the ornate mirror, then the reflected water stain on the ceiling.

My book bag is already zipped up when the bell rings. I'm the first out of Miss Numero Uno's classroom, and I trot down the wide wood planks of the hallway as quickly as I can without drawing attention to myself. Out the entrance, down the concrete steps, and onto the sidewalk, where I find my dad with his hands in his pockets, bouncing on his heels. He's like Mr. D with the heel-bouncing. Maybe it's a middle-aged-man thing. He gives me a grin that's almost a grimace. I've been mad at him ever since lunchtime, when I discovered he packed the most embarrassing lunch ever, but he's totally oblivious.

"Hey, honey. How was school?"

I hold up one finger to indicate *wait*. I rush down the sidewalk, and he picks up his pace to stay beside me.

We round the corner at the bodega, out of sight of school, and I drop my book bag to the sidewalk. I open my lunch box and pull out my sandwich.

"*This*," I say, "is how it was." I shake the bag so what's left of the hemp butter sandwich bounces inside it.

He cocks his head to the side. "I don't understand."

I growl. "You put my lunch in a dog poop bag! See? See the little dog grinning and giving a thumbs-up? This is what you bring to collect poop in when you take a dog for a walk. Why would you do that? Are you trying to ruin my life? Or just give everyone else at my school something to laugh about?"

"I think I can see your point." He's trying to look concerned and maybe sorry. But I can tell he thinks it's hilarious.

I drop the bag in a trash can. "It tasted exactly like what you'd expect to find in that bag."

"I sincerely promise that there was never any dog poop in there."

"It's called *the power of suggestion*. I read about it."

"Smarty-pants."

I close my lunch box. "Why do we even *have* dog poop bags?"

"A few years ago I thought it would be cool to take Meowzers on walks. Like a dog."

"I can imagine how that worked out." Meowzers won't even look out the window. He's strictly indoors.

"Meowzers did not wish to make it part of his fitness program."

"Anyway, I'm starving." I turn and look across the narrow street to a pizza joint. "So . . ."

"So you think I owe you a slice?"

"Or two. I'm a growing girl."

He smiles. Then he finally starts laughing. "I'm sorry, honey. I don't know where we keep the sandwich bags." He puts his arm around my shoulders as we walk across the street. "I'll figure it out."

I furrow my brow as he holds the door open at Luigi's Slices. "You don't really need to figure it out, right? I mean, Mom'll be back probably tomorrow. And Echo. Right?"

He smiles, but it's not a believable smile. He's never been good at hiding the truth.

Predictably, after pizza we drop down to the subway and head straight to the hospital. Dad says the idea is to get me to bed earlier, and also that there are certain people who work at the hospital who are there in the day and not in the evening after dinner. It sounds really fishy to me, and it makes me worry even more about this visit.

Arriving in Echo's room on the seventh floor, there are all sorts of doctors standing around. Everyone looks at me like I've interrupted a conversation I'm not supposed to hear.

A woman wearing surgical scrubs smiles at me. "You must be Echo's sister."

"Yes." I look around. Nobody says anything.

Echo is in her bed, asleep. She looks beaten-up, and her mouth is wide open. Her tumor is so huge it's practically coming out of her mouth.

"Is she okay?" I ask.

"Yes," Mom says. She doesn't look like she believes Echo is okay. "There's a person who'd like to meet with you, El. Why don't you go down to the lounge and she can come find you?"

Everyone is standing around waiting for me to leave. Mom and Dad, and three or four doctor types, and a nurse. It's like they're holding their breath.

"Okay," I say. I look over my shoulder at Echo as I begin leaving. Then I stop and glance at the monitors. The one that shows her heartbeat tells me her heart is still working. That will have to do for the moment.

I leave the room and walk down the hall to the lounge. It has tables and chairs, and a coffeemaker that makes tea and bad-smelling coffee, and a couch that faces a television, which shows a chubby man in silky shorts exercising with a bunch of old ladies. I'm just about to set down the tea I've made and join in the exercise routine when a round woman with a big smile walks into the lounge.

"You must be Echo's sister!"

"I must be," I say, then regret sounding snarky.

"Please, have a seat, and we'll chat."

I sit at a bleak table. She lowers herself across from me.

"I'm Jan," she says. "I'm so glad we finally get to meet! Your mother told me your name is Laughter. I love it!"

"She was joking," I say. "It's actually El."

"Oh. Okay. Well then, *El*, my job is to help family members of children who have cancer understand what they are going through, and also to help you become acquainted with the resources that are available to *you*."

"*Cancer?*" My mouth has been hanging open ever since she said that word. "I think you're confusing me with someone else. Nobody has said anything about my sister having cancer."

She straightens up and folds her hands on the table. "It *is* cancer, a very unusual variety called rhabdomyosarcoma. Only five children in every million will get it."

"My sister's name is Echo. She's got this thing in her mouth that's pushing her front teeth forward."

She nods. "Yes, that's the rhabdomyosarcoma. The tumor, you see. It's been growing very quickly. I know this is a shock—"

"Five kids in a million? Is that what you said? There's no way that Echo has that. She'd be more likely to be hit by lightning."

"Well, perhaps. But she *hasn't* been hit by lightning.

She has been—stricken—with rhabdomyosarcoma."

"Can you please stop saying that word?"

She inhales slowly and gets this expression like she's here to spread joy. "My job is to help you learn about it, and to help you and your parents become familiar with the resources that are available to you."

"You already said that!" My heart is beating fast, and my breathing is shallow. I reach into my shirt pocket for my tiny journal, flip through the pages without seeing what's written on them, then drop it in front of myself on the table, where it sits uselessly.

Jan takes a folder with the hospital's name on it from her canvas bag. She presents it to me.

"This is a bit of a starter kit I've compiled for you." She opens the folder. "This packet explains what rhabdomyosarcoma is. This one talks about the different types of treatments that are possible for Echo."

"Is she gonna be okay?"

"Well, your sister will get the best care possible. The doctors will work together to come up with—"

"Is she gonna live? Just tell me she's gonna live."

Jan folds her hands. She speaks like she's being careful with every word that comes out of her mouth. "There are many different factors that contribute to the survivability of cancer."

I bolt from my chair, which falls to the floor. I throw

my useless journal in the wastebasket on my way out of the lounge. I run down the hall to Echo's room. The conversation stops when I appear in the doorway.

"*El?*" Mom says.

"Why didn't you tell me? Why did you have that woman tell me?"

Mom looks to Dad, who looks back at her. I hurry to Echo's bed and put my hand on her arm. It's warm, and I can feel the life in her. Mom comes to my side and puts her arm around me, but I ignore her. Instead I look to the monitor, which shows Echo's heart beat, beat, beat.

5

FRIDAY MORNING I wake up and cry. It's the first thing I do. I think of the empty bed in the bunk below me. I think of it being empty forever. I think of Echo's birthday coming and her not being around to celebrate it. I think of vacations without her, and Christmas, and Halloween. There's no way we can do any of those things happily without her. We were a family of three before she came along, and it was fine. But I don't want to go back to being a family of three.

We can never be three again. It's not fair to Echo. It's not fair to me.

The jackhammers and power tools come alive to mark the hour of seven, Echo's age at her next birthday. I think of how much the universe would suck if

Echo wasn't able to make it to her seventh birthday. Then Dad raps on the door and opens it.

He looks at me, gauges me. "Good morning."

"That's a generous assessment."

He nods. "I'll give you one free pass from school. Do you want to make it today?"

"Yes."

He nods again. "Okay. I'll make breakfast."

He shuts the door. I lie on my bed and hear him calling the school. Two schools, actually—mine and Echo's. Then I hear the skillet and the coffeemaker, all in between the jackhammer and the saws and all the other racket.

I smell pancakes through the vent, but it doesn't connect to my stomach. I smell the coffee, hear the teapot whistle, but it doesn't get me out of bed. Finally he comes for me.

"You'll have to eat something," he says.

At the table, I pick at my pancakes. Instead of cutting them into fat bites with my knife, I shred them with my fork.

The classical station is on the radio, but it's pointless with the noise of construction and destruction from outside and next door. Meowzers jumps from a chair to the table. He looks at me, sees my expression, and jumps back to the floor.

"I'm hoping you can help me with something," Dad says.

"What." I ask it without a lilt.

"This is going to be hard on all of us. But we can get through it together. And in the spirit of that idea, I've devised a cheesy slogan."

"Oh." I really meant that as *Oh?* It just didn't come out that way.

"The slogan is 'All for one, all four one.'"

I take a sip of tea. "That's kinda redundant."

He leans forward. "No, the second four is the *number* four. Like, all four of us are—"

"I get it," I say. "I was just kidding." I take another sip of tea. "It's really kinda sweet."

"The tea?"

"No, your slogan. I think it's nice."

He sits up straight. "*Thank* you. So, I was hoping you could make a sign. Something to motivate us as a family and remind us that we're in this together. And I thought you could do it since your lettering is so good. Like, we could get a chalkboard, and you could write that slogan, and all the other things we need to do. Like eat right."

"We already eat right."

65

"Well, we can eat even *more* right." Dad gestures to the plate in front of him. "Like, this breakfast doesn't have any color in it."

I yawn. "Sleep right."

"Yeah, and exercise. And what else?"

I raise my cup for another sip but pause before it hits my lips. "Laughter."

"Ha! Yes, laughter. Laughter is the best medicine."

"Good luck with that one." I take another sip. "Maybe we need a bunch of funny movies."

"That's not a bad idea. We can ask everyone for their favorites."

"And funny books." I try a bite of the pancake.

"We'll get a chalkboard sign from the art supply store," Dad says. "And you can write all these things down and make it look fancy."

"I can use different-colored chalk."

"Yes!"

"And four colors of chalk will defeat cancer and restore Echo's health."

Dad's smile disappears. He reaches over to me and touches my arm. "Stay positive. That's the most important thing to put on the chalkboard. *Stay positive.*"

"Okay."

"And pick each other up when one of us is down."

"Okay."

The room gets quiet, except for the sound outside of concrete being beaten to dust and wood being shredded and splintered next door.

"I'm kinda down right now," I say.

Dad pushes away from the table and kneels beside my chair, his arm around me.

"Everything is going to be okay," he says.

The room is blurry with my tears. "I don't want *everything* to be okay. I just want *Echo* to be okay."

But he can't tell me Echo is going to be okay. He can't tell me because he's terrible at lying, or saying things he isn't sure are true. So he just hugs me tighter, and that'll have to do for now.

After breakfast we go to the Jefferson Market Library. It's my favorite, but it's a little less my favorite without Echo. She loves the children's section and the spiral stairs, and her love is contagious. We get a couple of new books for her, to help her pass the time in the hospital.

Then we go to the art supply store to get a small chalkboard—which is also magnetic—and colored chalk, and some extra magnets so we can hang pictures on the board. We gather it all and bring it to the register.

"Tate!" says the man at the register, a guy my dad's age. "How is Echo?"

Dad smiles. "She's hanging tough. She's a brave little girl."

The man looks at me. "Hello, El!"

"Hello," I say. I can't remember his name, but he always remembers mine.

The guy leans toward Dad and lowers his tone.

"We're all thinkin' about Echo. Listen, you've spent so much money on paint here over the years, back in the day. Let's say this is on us. Our way of saying thanks."

"You sure?"

The man puts our stuff in a bag. "It's nothing. Hey, you know what, we'll put out a jar for people to put their change in. Or whatever they can. To help with expenses."

Dad puts his free hand on his heart. "That's very thoughtful of you."

"We'll keep Echo in our thoughts." He looks at me. "*All* of you guys. You're some of the good people in the neighborhood. Everyone knows that."

"Thank you." Dad smiles. "See you soon."

I don't frown until we're outside the store. I think of my new status—Echo's sister, the other kid in the charity case family—the whole way home.

When we get to our apartment I do the chalkboard

sign, and it sort of cheers me up even though it makes me cry. I'm not sure how that works.

ALL FOR ONE—ALL FOUR ONE
eat right—sleep well—exercise—
laugh—pick each other up when one
of us is down—stay positive!

Dad asks me to pick some fun photographs for the board, which I put in the corners.

There's one of Echo on the Central Park carousel, on a summer day when she was five and finally agreed to ride the carousel without Dad standing beside her, only because he bribed her with the promise of ice cream afterward. There's one of her on her first day of kindergarten, standing by the door with her first-day-of-school dress, smiling with tears in her eyes. The third photo shows her wearing a party hat on her sixth birthday, just before she locked herself in the bathroom after she got scared by the ventriloquist doll, Splinters, that entertained the guests. The last one shows all four of us—Mom, Dad, Echo, and me—sitting on a bench at Rockefeller Center with the giant Christmas tree behind. It's the picture we used for our holiday greeting card last year.

By the time I'm done looking through pictures, remembering everything as I choose which ones to use, I feel really ready to see her. Being away from Echo makes my heart ache.

Dad fixes each of us a grilled cheese for lunch. I remind him that we're supposed to eat right, so he adds sliced tomatoes and avocado, which makes it taste amazing. He cuts it diagonally, and I have it with a cold glass of hemp milk.

After lunch, we walk down into the subway station, where again we see the piano guy. He's playing an old jazz song called "Let's Get Lost" as we walk onto the platform. Getting lost—as the song suggests—sounds like a great idea, but I'm stuck in the real world.

Dad looks down the track like the train is gonna come roaring in and we'll have to jump on it as it passes. He's pretending not to notice the piano guy.

"I love this song," I say.

He turns to me. "So do I."

I nod my head to the tune. "He plays it really well."

Dad smiles absently. "He certainly does."

I try laying on the guilt. "It's nice to hear a piano, since we don't have one in our living room anymore. Well, except that little keyboard in the closet."

Dad looks away from me, back down the track into the tunnel to the south. When his gaze returns to me, I'm snapping my fingers. Dad rolls his eyes and reaches for his wallet.

"Honey, this has gotta be the last time for the near future." He hands me a one-dollar bill. "We have to start being very careful with money. It's just . . ."

I wait, but he doesn't finish his thought. So I run to the piano guy and fold the bill twice before dropping it into his jar. Again he smiles, and when he smiles I know this is the best I'm going to feel all day. At this moment everything is right in the universe. But then the train roars into the station and its brakes scream, drowning out the tune, and it's time to run back to Dad and jump on.

The subway door slides shut and we roll away into the dark. I look at my illuminated reflection in the window across from me and think of a time when Echo was small, maybe two. Dad gave her a dollar to tip a saxophone player at Washington Square, but she was always so shy she just wanted to keep the dollar herself. She finally summoned the courage to approach him, but after dropping the dollar in she reached in and grabbed a handful of bills and toddled away.

I was really embarrassed by Echo, but I wasn't too much older than she is now. The sax player thought it was funny, but only because he eventually got his money back. Now, rolling in the dark tunnel, seeing myself reflected in the train window, I look sad. I look like I wish my biggest worry about my little sister was being embarrassed by her.

"So, Echo had a procedure this morning." Dad's words bring me back from my reflection in the train window.

"A procedure?"

"A small, minor surgery."

"Did they remove the tumor?"

"No, they installed a port in her chest. It connects to her bloodstream so they can put the medicine in every week. They want to shrink the tumor for about twelve weeks with the chemotherapy, and *then* do surgery to remove the tumor."

"So, everything is gonna be okay?"

He smiles, but again it isn't convincing. "The medicine will make her feel really sick. It'll make her hair fall out and some other nasty side effects. But it'll work on the tumor. Shrinking it before cutting it out means a smaller hole in the roof of her mouth and hopefully fewer teeth missing."

That hits me like a punch in the stomach. Then he tells me that as an added bonus the medicine will make her immune system very weak, so she will get sick easily and not be able to get better easily when she does get sick. So we all have to wash our hands constantly to keep germs away from her, and if any one of the rest of us gets sick, that person will have to stay somewhere else until they get better. He says a flu shot is the first thing on the menu when we walk out of the hospital.

This all sounds so awful. But part of me is anxious for it to begin, because the tumor is growing so fast I'm afraid it will take over her whole head. And what would that mean? If there has to be a fight I want it to begin now. I want them to let Echo take her first swing at her foe.

I think all of this as we walk from the subway to the hospital, and after we arrive, watching her lying in her hospital bed. The IV is still hooked up to her arm for now, and her head is lolled to the side. Every few seconds I glance to the monitor to watch her heart beat, beat, beat.

I remember when Mom was pregnant with Echo, and Dad and I came with her to a doctor's appointment. The doctor had a wand held against Mom's belly and moved it around until the sound of Echo's heart beating filled the room. I remember seeing Dad smile.

There it is, he said. *Long may you run.*

Now it's less than seven years later, and already there's a worry.

Echo hasn't been allowed to eat since last night at

midnight, or drink any water, because of the surgery to install the port in her chest. It's just below her collarbone on her right side. When she wakes up she'll be starving and thirsty. And in pain.

I can hear Dad talking on his phone by the window. He's got his back to me, but I can hear his side of the conversation.

"That doesn't make any sense. What good is a network if there isn't anyone capable of doing that surgery in the network?"

He turns from the window to look at Mom, who sits with her sketch folio in the stiff-backed chair. She stares at him hopelessly.

Dad turns back to the window. "What are we paying for every month, then?"

He puts his hand to his forehead. He looks defeated. "Well, you people need to figure it out. Get it in front of the person who makes the exceptions. The reason for exceptions is that if you don't have someone in network who can do it then you get someone out of the network. And this—this isn't something that can wait." He hangs up his cell phone and puts it in his pocket, then turns to Mom. I look to the TV screen, but it isn't on.

"Have you talked to Ingrid today?" He's referring to Mom's boss.

Instead of answering him, Mom speaks to me. "El,

can you do me a favor and run down to the first floor and get me a cappuccino? You can get something for yourself, too."

I act happy. "Cool. Do you want anything, Dad?"

"No thanks."

Mom gives me a ten-dollar bill. "Four-shot cappuccino, please."

I smile and head out the door. The nurses' station is right across from the door, so I can't stand and lurk in the hallway to eavesdrop, but I *can* kneel down to tie my shoe, and that is what I do.

Mom speaks quietly. "Ingrid left me about ten voice messages while Echo was in surgery."

I untie my left shoe and slowly redo it with big bows.

"What did she say?" Dad asks.

"She said I needed to decide if the job was important to me."

I untie my right shoe, slowly.

"Did you call her back? What did you say?"

"I told her that caring for Echo was what was important to me right now."

Slowly I make the bows for the right shoe.

"I take it that didn't end well?"

"No." Mom sounds stricken.

I pull the laces tight and hurry quietly away.

Down the hall I wait for the elevator. I look out the big window at midtown Manhattan, at the tall buildings of this strange, scary city. It's the same city I've always known, but now it seems sinister and deadly.

If Mom doesn't have a job, that leaves us with Dad working part-time as an after-school art instructor, teaching five-year-olds how to paint. That's what he's been doing while working on getting a master's degree so he can teach college students how to paint for much more money.

I remember when everything changed. We were having pancakes at the breakfast table on a Saturday morning. We call it the "breakfast table" but it's the only table in our tiny apartment, and we eat every meal there. It's in the kitchen, which is so small you can practically reach the silverware drawer without getting up from your chair.

Dad took a sip from his coffee cup and set it down. "Mommy and I have some exciting news."

I looked from Dad to Mom and swallowed my bite of pancake. "What is it?"

"We're getting a dog!" Echo shouted.

I looked to Echo, then Mom. "Are we?"

Mom smiled. "No. Meowzers would have none of that."

"A rabbit!"

"It's quite a lot bigger than that," Dad said. Then he looked to Mom.

"A bear!"

"Echo, stop!" I said. She didn't really think we would be getting a bear, but she's always being ridiculous.

"Not a bigger pet," Mom said. "Bigger news."

I looked from her to Dad and back. "Are you having a baby?"

Mom smiled but shook her head. Neither of them seemed to be dying to spill the news, whatever it was.

Finally Dad took another sip of coffee and spoke. "Ingrid, who is Mommy's biggest customer, has offered Mommy a position."

I sat against my chairback. "What do you mean?"

"That means," Mom began, "that instead of selling her the dresses I've made, I'm going to be designing dresses for her, which will then be made by other people. And that means better pay. And security."

"And benefits," Dad added. "After six months."

Echo looked extremely disappointed. She returned to eating her pancake.

"What else?" I asked. Because I knew that wasn't everything.

Mom took a bite of pancake and spoke to her plate. "Remember when your dad and I showed you where we went to school for junior high and high school? The Village Arts Academy?"

"Yes."

I watched her. She continued to act like the pancakes were the most important thing on her mind, but I knew they weren't.

"Well," she said, "now that we'll have a bigger income, we'll be able to send you there." She finally met my eyes. "If that's still your wish."

"Yes!" It was definitely still my wish. At least I thought it was.

Dad cleared his throat. "As long as they give the legacy discount to children of former students who got kicked out the week before graduating."

My jaw dropped.

"Don't worry," Mom said. "*One* of us left the school in good standing. Meaning *me.*"

Mom looked to Dad, who quickly put a forkful of pancake into his mouth.

A worry entered my head. "What about Maisy? What about all my other friends?"

Dad threw his hands into the air. "You can make new friends!" He said it like it was a glorious idea.

"What your father means," Mom said, "is that you can still be friends with all the girls you know from your current school, but you can also meet new friends at the academy."

"And what about tennis?" I asked. "You said they don't do sports at the academy."

"No problem." Dad dismissed my concern with a wave of his hand. "We can sign you up for a city league."

Then Mom looked directly at me and put a pleasant expression on her face. "Also, instead of making dresses in the living room and selling them to Ingrid and other boutiques, I'll be going to her studio in the Garment District every day."

"What about Meowzers?" Echo asked. "He'll be lonely!"

"Meowzers is gonna love having the apartment to himself!" Dad turned in his chair. "Look at him! He heard us talking about it and came in to say how excited he is!"

We all looked to Meowzers, who stood stiffly by the refrigerator. We watched as his stomach convulsed, and he made a terrible hacking sound as he threw up a hairball on the kitchen floor.

Of course everything hasn't turned out great. My beloved tennis is now once every week at the tennis center instead of every day at school. My other favorite activity, playing the piano, hasn't gotten any easier.

Even with Mom's dress forms stored away now that she's working at Ingrid's studio instead of in our living room, the keyboard still has to go back into the closet every time I finish playing. Our piano teacher moved to France at the beginning of summer, and Mom and Dad were talking about finding a new one. But I'm sure that will never happen now.

Worst, over the summer, after I found out I would be going to a different school, the friends I had became the friends I *once* had, because people prefer friends they get to see every day. I feel like when they reach out to me with texts they're doing it because they feel sorry for me or because their moms made them. My mom says I'm imagining it, that of course they still want to be friends with me. And now, with Echo being sick and getting this terrible diagnosis, answering texts and talking about my miserable new life is the last thing I want to do.

As if on cue, my cell phone buzzes in my clenched hand. I look from Echo's heart monitor to the screen. It's another text from Maisy.

Can't wait to hear about your new school! Does Echo like first grade?

I text back a quick lie.

Everything's great! So busy. Talk soon!

I'm tired of wondering about the answers to my own questions, let alone questions from Maisy or anyone else. I'm tired of pretending things are okay, and I don't want to say how they really are.

The elevator dings, bringing me back to this moment. The doors open and I wonder how long I've been standing here, how many elevators have come and gone while my mind wandered. I get on, the doors close, and tears pour from my eyes. I watch the numbers light as I descend from seven to one, then wipe my eyes before the doors open again.

While waiting in line to get Mom's four-shot cappuccino and a blended ice-cream drink for myself, I think about every nightmare scenario of us living on the streets and begging for food while Echo's tumor grows. I imagine the surgery being performed by a guy with a rusty blade beneath a bridge over the Hudson River. If Dad doesn't win whatever argument he's having on his desperate phone calls with the insurance company, I don't know how it's going to end up any better than that.

I order and give the ten to the cashier. The change is less than a dollar. I drop one penny in the tip jar to make some noise and put the rest in my jeans pocket.

When I get off the elevator back to the seventh floor, my phone buzzes. Another text from Maisy.

El! Have you been abducted by aliens? Lol. We need to get together!

I stare at the screen, at her words. I set the drinks on the counter at the nurses' station and reply.

Lol! Yes, aliens who like assigning a ton of homework. Mainly rocket science and astrophysics of course. Yes let's get together soon!

Back at the room I hear Echo's voice as I enter. "Where's El?"

I come in with a drink in each hand. Mom puts down her folio and stands, comes to Echo's side.

"She's here, honey. How do you feel?"

"I feel like I've been in a spaceship. What did the aliens do to me?"

Mom smiles. "They put the port in, remember?"

"But not aliens," Dad says. "The doctors."

"Hi, Echo," I say, and hand Mom's cappuccino to her. "I've missed you."

"I've missed you, too."

"I was here yesterday but you were asleep."

The nurse comes in, this time a guy with a shaved head. "Hello, Sleeping Beauty. How do you feel?"

"Good."

"Any pain? Does it hurt anywhere?"

"No."

"Awesome. I just need to take your vitals." He puts the blood pressure cuff around her arm.

"El, tell me what you think of this." Mom picks up her folio and turns it around to show me. It's a drawing of a dress. The proportions indicate that it's for a little girl. Mom points at the drawing with her pencil.

"This is a flap for accessing the port. So if a girl has to have chemo and she wants to wear a dress, she can. She doesn't have to take the dress off or lower it off her shoulder while she's getting treatment."

Another feature of our new, grim reality. But Mom is smiling, and the new rule is *stay positive*, so I smile back. "Cool."

"I thought I could make a dress like this for Echo. And if it works, maybe I could make more and try to sell them."

"Doesn't somebody already do that?"

Mom closes her folio and sets it on the nightstand by Echo's bed. "Well, they do, but what I've seen looks mainly . . . *institutional*. Like it was issued by a hospital instead of bought at a cute boutique."

"Everything looks beautiful," the nurse says, taking the cuff off Echo's arm. "Are you ready for a Popsicle?"

"*Yes!*" Echo has officially woken up.

"Great. I'll be right back."

"Anyway," Mom continues, "remember what it was like when I used to have my own dress studio?"

"Of course. In our living room."

"Yes. Well, Echo is not going to be able to go to school for a while. At least a few months, until after the winter break. So being able to work from home is very appealing right now."

"Did Ingrid fire you?"

She clears her throat. "I told Ingrid I would not be able to meet her demands."

Dad stands from the bench by the window. "When one door closes, another door opens."

I look to him. He moves his hands upward in a lifting motion while making a face at me.

"Right," I say. "That sounds really cool." Dad gives me a thumbs-up for being positive.

"Popsicles!" Echo shouts. The nurse has come in holding two. One for Echo and one for me.

We eat them together, and I watch her. She looks like she can taste the sweet of the Popsicle, but I can only feel the cold.

6

SATURDAY MORNING I wake up before Dad. It's been only one week of school but already I am in the habit of waking up too early. The jackhammer has taken the weekend off, as have all the other noisemakers. But I'm up early anyway.

Saturday I get to whack balls at the tennis center and destroy my opponent in the Hudson Juniors League, so I get out of bed even though I'm tired. I make myself toast and veggie sausage and a pot of strong tea to split with Dad. He does coffee on weekdays but always tea on weekends, because weekends are supposed to be slower. I'm just finishing up my breakfast when he drags himself into the kitchen.

"Good morning," I say through a mouthful of toast. "There's tea."

"Thanks."

Then I hoist the tennis racquet that's been lying across my lap and wave it at him.

Dad gives a grim smile as he sits at the table. "About that," he says.

"What?"

He fills his teacup from the shiny kettle. Steam rises. "I know how much you love tennis."

This isn't going to end well.

"And it's a great thing in every respect." He bounces his tea bag up and down in the water. "The exercise, the stress relief."

"The feeling good about gracefully destroying the girl on the other side of the net."

"Yes." He smiles. "But right now, with Echo in the hospital, and then getting treatment every Thursday—which will probably result in her feeling poorly through Saturdays—and the distance, and the expense . . ."

"Are you saying I can't do tennis anymore?"

"Just temporarily." He reaches for my arm. "I'm sorry, El."

I pull my arm away. If I can't have tennis, he can't have my arm.

"I know how disappointing this is," he says. "But I was thinking maybe we could throw the Frisbee together. It's relaxing, the motion is like your backhand in tennis. And we can throw outside on the street so we don't have to spend half the day going somewhere to do it."

"Playing on the street sucks. It always goes down into stairwells."

"Then maybe we can play catch with a baseball."

"Remember the broken car window?"

"Oh, I remember all right." He smiles again. "We could use a tennis ball instead."

"Great. That'll remind me of what I'm missing out on."

He takes another sip of tea. "It isn't the end of tennis, just like it isn't the end of school for Echo. She'll be back to school one day, and you'll be back to playing tennis."

He had to frame it in terms of Echo's cancer to make me feel guilty about moping over not playing tennis. Like he won't be happy until everyone in the family is suffering in equal measure.

One for all, all four one.

The session of throwing the tennis ball isn't as awful as I'd expected. The ball feels good in my hands as I throw and catch, and I realize my body has been tightly wound with stress. This is why *exercise* is one of the elements listed on the All Four One board.

Also, the street is quieter on weekends. And New York City in September can be about as pretty as any-place.

Echo drifts in and out of my mind. When Echo is in my mind it's not happy Echo thoughts. When Echo *isn't* in my mind it doesn't matter what it is—

Trees, wearing their September green.

Tennis ball traveling back and forth between my Dad and me.

Old lady walking a tiny dog with an eye patch down the sidewalk.

Like very short days alternating between the dark-ness of night and the light of day, my head fills with a few seconds of Echo having cancer, then gives way to a few seconds of anything else.

Dad carries the All Four One chalkboard as we walk to the subway in the early afternoon. We head to the station south of the Jefferson Market Library, but first Dad wants to stop at a healthy market for a vitality juice with turmeric. By *vitality* they mean disgusting, and I don't know how he thinks Echo will be per-suaded to drink it. But he means well, so I don't tell him it's hopeless.

I can hear the piano as we descend the stairs to the tracks. My heart sinks. I don't want to stand listening to the piano guy play so beautifully and not be able to tip him.

I pause halfway down. "Maybe we should walk? We can save money. It's a nice day and it'll be good exercise."

Dad shakes his head. "Not this time. I've got too much stuff to carry. And it's a *long* walk. We've got a busy day."

I roll my eyes. Then I remember we can't afford any of us being negative, so I roll them back and continue downstairs toward the trains going north and the trains going south, and the piano on the platform between the tracks.

We have to walk right by him. He's playing something a hundred years old by Scott Joplin, way beyond my ability. It's called "Solace," and it's heartbreakingly beautiful, even with the terrible acoustics of the subway station. We have to stand close by, because it wouldn't make sense to walk away from him.

I loved taking piano lessons, even though I wasn't terribly good. Echo picked it up better than me. Of course now there's no possibility of Mom and Dad paying for lessons. A southbound train comes and overpowers the Joplin song. Then the train stops, and "Solace" returns. I feel guilty that I'm enjoying it and we can't tip, but it was Dad's money anyway. And like Dad says, most people don't tip.

But maybe most people don't enjoy it the way I do.

I glance at the piano guy and he smiles. I smile back and look away. But from the corner of my eye he beckons me over. I look at Dad, then down the track. The train isn't coming along to force me away, so I walk with guilty feet to the piano guy.

"Hey!" he says. He finishes the song. "Have you got a request? You guys tip me so often but you never ask for anything."

"No, thank you."

"Come on. *Anything*. If you don't like this old stuff, I also know songs that kids your age typically like."

"I liked that last song. It's just what I needed to hear."

"Thanks! That was Scott Joplin."

"I know."

He brightens. "You do? Do you play?"

"I used to take lessons. We have a keyboard, but our apartment is so small it's always put away in a closet."

He laughs. "Yeah, my piano fits much better down here and up in Washington Square than it does in my apartment. But I have to drag it back every night anyway. Or earlier in the day if the cops show up and ask if I've got a permit." He bangs on the keys. "But don't leave your keyboard in the closet. Take it out and let it sing."

I fold my hands. "I'm not very good."

"Keep at it. You'll thank yourself later."

"I have a hard time with the left hand."

He scratches his scruffy chin. "We could play together. Your right hand, my left."

I smile. Then I look over my shoulder at the uptown C train as it screeches in. "Maybe next time."

"Give me an exit theme." He looks like he won't take no for an answer.

"'Everything Happens to Me.'"

He puts his hand to his chest. "Ah! A girl after my own heart. Moments like this give me the strength to drag my piano around every day. See you later, alligator."

He begins playing it, sweet and sad, and a little funny. I watch the piano guy over my shoulder as I hurry to Dad, and the piano guy watches me back. Dad and I jump on the train, and the doors close.

I hear the song in my head as the train enters the tunnel. My fists unclench, my fingers twitch. And then, even though the people on the subway might think I'm weird for doing it, I spread my hands wide to play the tune on an invisible keyboard.

It sounds perfect.

When Dad and I arrive at the hospital, they have already begun Echo's first round of chemo. Dad puts his hand on the IV bag dripping not into her arm but into the port buried beneath the skin on the right side of her chest. Dad's head tips down, he closes his eyes. He almost looks like he's praying.

"Do your thing," he says quietly to the bag of chemo. "Show no mercy."

For some reason this immediately makes tears well up in my eyes.

But Echo thinks all of this is hilarious. "Look, I'm a robot," she says, and does a robot dance.

But she can't really do a robot dance, since she's stuck in bed connected to a tube stuck into her chest. So instead she just moves her arms stiffly like robots are expected to do when they dance.

Mom leaves the hospital for a while, which stinks because I've hardly seen her at all this week. But she needs a break from being stuck in the room with Echo. Not so much being stuck in here with Echo, just being stuck *here*. So she goes home, where she hasn't been since Monday, and runs a couple of errands.

Echo isn't terribly excited about the All Four One

chalkboard. But she's excited that Dad brought the first Harry Potter book to read to her. He sits beside her bed and finds the first page of text.

"I read this to El starting when she was your age," he tells her. "It took about eighteen months to get through all of the books, so we should be finishing the series just before your eighth birthday."

I know he's making a point of being optimistic. Underneath any statement like that is the worry that she won't live to be that age. But staying positive, as he said, is the most important thing.

"Where was I when you read it to El?" she asks.

"You were asleep. But now you're a big kid, so you can handle these books."

Echo's terribly excited to learn she's following in my footsteps. She gets comfortable, arranging around herself the stuffed animals people have brought or had delivered. I turn off the TV.

Dad holds the book at arm's length. In his voice I can hear him get choked up as the first words come to his lips.

"Chapter One. The Boy . . . Who *Lived*."

First hour on Monday, while waiting for Mr. D's class to begin, I'm holding my breath and watching the clock on the wall. Tick, tick, tick. Every second I can hold my breath is another year of life granted to Echo. If I can hold it a minute and a half it means a pretty long life for her. I realize it's a ridiculous superstition, but it's no worse than stepping on a crack and breaking your mother's back.

Thirty seconds. Tick, tick, tick.

"Hey!" It's the girl to my left. Sydney. "Your lips look so cute. Is that glitter in your lip gloss?"

I look at her, then up to the clock on the wall.

Tick, tick, tick.

Sydney is turned in her seat, facing me. "I have raspberry lip gloss if you ever want to try. Unless you think it's gross to share."

I look at her lips, then up at the clock on the wall.

Tick, tick, tick.

"Is that silver glitter in yours?" She looks so eager.

I touch my lips with my index finger, and hold it away to look at it. Then I glance back up at the clock on the wall. Sixty seconds.

"It's so cute." She searches my face, waiting for a response.

But I cannot respond, even if she thinks I'm being rude or weird. Not until at least ninety seconds. All I can do is smile weakly, my lips tight to keep my breath in.

"Anyway. I like Emily Dickinson too. But my favorite poet is—"

The bell rings, interrupting her. Sydney's face shows disappointment as she turns away.

Mr. D walks back and forth at the front of the classroom in short paces. He's wearing khaki pants and a sweater-vest, holding our assignments in a big folder.

With a sharp gasp, I take in a new breath. Mr. D stops pacing, smiles at me curiously, then begins addressing the class.

"Good morning, everyone. Did you all have a nice weekend?"

A few kids mumble yes or no. I don't feel like I've had a weekend at all. And I was only able to hold my breath for seventy-nine seconds.

"First I'd like to hand back your writing assignment, 'Theater of Emotion.'"

I'm dreading getting the assignment back because I know I did a terrible job on it. Mr. D assigned it on Thursday, and then a few hours later I found out that Echo has cancer. I couldn't concentrate on the assignment at all, and I had to email it to Mr. D on Friday since I missed school. As a result my work was pretty much a joke. So I sit at my desk pretending to look in my book bag because I don't want him to see my eyes.

"It always amazes me to see the variety of work that a class can produce when given a fairly open-ended assignment." He starts moving up and down the aisles, dropping papers onto desks. "In this case, *Write a movie scene where the character is dealing with strong emotions.*"

He drops a paper in front of the girl who sits to the left of me. Sydney. She scowls at her grade.

"Not only was there great diversity in the subject matter," Mr. D continues, "and what the characters in your stories experienced, but also the manner in which you executed it."

I start biting my nails. Up and down the aisles he goes.

"There was some excellent work, and some that could have been stronger. But there was one student whose effort showed me bravery, creativity, and an unusual understanding of the subject matter."

I am overcome with dread as I realize there is only one paper he hasn't handed back, and I am the only student who hasn't been handed a paper. He takes his reading glasses from his shirt pocket, puts them on, and looks to the paper in his hand.

"This student describes a scene where, for several pages, an adolescent girl lies motionless in bed, in a

room lit by daylight. On and on it goes with no move-
ment or action from the girl. Just the clock ticking,
the sounds of cars and trucks going by outside, and a
pigeon on the windowsill cooing and sharpening his
claws on the ledge. As a reader I started to wonder
whether the girl was dead or alive. But just when I
began to wonder that, the narrator makes mention of
the girl's body temperature and pulse."

Mr. D laughs, and the pages shake in his hand. I
switch hands in my nail-biting.

"Then, finally, the girl's phone buzzes. She rolls
over, reaches for it, and ignores a text message from
someone described as her last remaining friend. Then
after a minute she gets up and goes to the bathroom.
The narrator describes the pigeon looking through
the window into the empty bedroom, tilting his head
with curiosity." Laughter from the class. "Then the
girl shuffles back into the room and to the bed with an
empty expression. She lies down and presumably goes
back to sleep, or at least lies there motionless. After
another two pages of inaction the scene ends abruptly
and without resolution."

My jaw is clenched. I'm legitimately horrified.

But Mr. D looks down at me, his eyes shining.

"Well done, Miss El." He drops the stapled pages on
my desk. "Well done."

My face burns as I stare down at the *105 percent* written in red ink.

"How is that an expression of strong emotion?" It's Sydney. She looks furious, like it's a tremendous injustice that I've been given a high mark.

Mr. D raises an eyebrow and looks to me. "El, would you like to respond to Sydney's question?" I *wouldn't* like to respond to Sydney's question, and I *don't* respond to it immediately, so he adds, "What emotion do you think is on display in your piece?"

I don't look up. "Grief." I say it flatly. But I immediately regret saying it flatly and not looking up, because now I look like *I'm* the one suffering from grief. And I *am* the one suffering from grief.

So now I'm the grief-stricken girl. That's probably how all the kids will look at me. And that isn't the look I'm going for.

This is now officially the worst year ever. Of school, of my life. I wish I could go to sleep and wake up when it's over.

When the bell rings at the end of class my backpack is already zipped. I'm ready to turn away from it. But I hear Mr. D's voice over my shoulder.

"El, can I have a word with you?"

I pretend not to hear. I know he's going to ask me if everything's okay.

"El?"

I disappear into the throng of students heading to the door. I glance in his direction as I leave the classroom. Sydney is standing directly in front of him, talking to him, keeping him away from me. He looks over her and meets my eyes just before I disappear.

7

UNFORTUNATELY I *DON'T* get to sleep through the school year, or my life. Instead it drags on, friendless and dreadful. I try to pour myself into the homework, because it's the only part of my life where I have any control over the outcome.

It's now Wednesday, the twenty-second day since Echo went into the hospital. She's been home for exactly two weeks. And by home I mean *home.* She can't go to school because all the snotty, germy first-grade kids are a threat to her weakened immune system. Instead her teacher comes two or three evenings each week for a couple of hours to keep her caught up. The only places Echo goes are chemo appointments and the emergency room, where she's gone twice when her temperature was too high. That's the protocol.

I'm at school, sitting alone in the cafeteria, eating a sandwich that I cannot taste. I don't mind eating alone because it's easier than pretending I'm happy.

Next item, carrot sticks. My parents are even more crazy about nutrition since Echo got cancer, even though eating healthy didn't do Echo a bit of good. We've always eaten healthy but she got cancer anyway.

The bright gray light from the windows gets less bright, and I look up. Octavius is standing across the table from me, blocking the windows.

"Hey," he says.

I would say *hey* back, with even less enthusiasm than he did, but my mouth is full of assorted lunch items that I'm trying to get down. So I give a little wave that looks like the windshield wipers of a car going across the window just once.

He holds a tray of cafeteria food. He evidently eats whatever it is they're serving. "So, I have a confession."

I watch him and wait but he's apparently going to make me ask him. *"What?"* My question is half muffled by bread.

"You know how the first week of school I said I wanted to get a bracelet—one like you were wearing— for my girlfriend?"

I remember, but I shrug like I don't.

"Well," he says, "I don't actually have a girlfriend."

I swallow my bite. "Obviously."

He looks maybe a little bit hurt.

"Sorry," I say. "I just meant that I never saw you with one."

He nods. "Well, I'm glad that I have that cleared up. Enjoy your lunch."

He begins to turn away.

"Wait—"

He stops and looks back to me.

I clear my throat. "I have a *series* of confessions to make."

He stands and waits. The smell of cafeteria food washes over me and makes me feel slightly ill.

"One—you told me to enjoy my lunch, but I do *not* enjoy my lunch."

"The cafeteria food isn't bad. You should try it."

"It's not the food that keeps me from enjoying it." I clear my throat again. "Two—my grandmother is not the person who was being treated at Midtown Children's Hospital."

"That's not much of a confession. Obviously they don't treat grandmothers at Midtown Children's Hospital. Unless it's the nine-year-old grandmother I read about in the *Global Inquisitor.*"

I almost smile. If I ever open up to anyone, it may as well be this boy, who's almost funny. Maybe under different circumstances he'd be full-on funny. So I take a deep breath. "Three—my little sister, Echo, has cancer."

His expression changes, but just a little, like the clouds the sun is hiding behind got thicker and darker. This is the moment he decides he doesn't want to be around the sad-case girl, the depressed girl, and turns and walks away so he can sit with happy kids.

But he doesn't turn away. "I knew it was cancer," he says. "Your bracelet is a seventh-floor bracelet. That's where the kids with compromised immune systems are."

"Yes."

"Which is almost always from chemotherapy."

"I know," I say.

He's still standing there with his tray in his hands. The gravy on his chicken-fried steak is coagulating, wrinkling. "You need to stay positive. You need to be optimistic and surround yourself with people who are gonna make you believe that everything will turn out okay."

I can tell he's going to say something more, so I wait.

"You should stay away from me," he says, and turns away again.

"Wait!" I say it so loud this time, everyone in the cafeteria looks at me. Octavius comes back. "Just please sit with me," I say. "Okay? You can't make my reality worse than it already is just by sitting with me, because I already know the worst thing that can happen." I feel like the whole cafeteria is listening to me, but I say it anyway. "I just want you to sit with me."

He lowers his tray and sits down across from me. I feel like maybe he'd smile if not for the miserable expression on my face. I wish I could tell him it's okay if he wants to smile.

"Thank you," I say. Then my face comes apart as I eat the rest of my lunch, tears pouring into the corners of my mouth and sheeting off my cheeks, but I don't look down. I don't hide my face, my tears. I keep eating, because eating right is one of the tenets of the stupid slogan my dad made up. And because I'm used to crying by now, and because Dad forgot to put a napkin in my lunch, so there's nothing I can use to wipe the tears away. Last, I don't hide my tears because I've just chosen this strangely charming boy as my confidante. And tears are nothing between confidantes.

We don't talk at all. He eats his disgusting cafeteria food and I eat my flavorless lunch. But it feels good to not be alone.

Miss Numero Uno watches the class filing into seventh-hour art from a stool by the clay. She's wearing high heels and skinny black jeans beneath a black sweater that's partially covered by a paint-splattered apron. She's drawn her eyebrows with what looks like an even thicker stick of charcoal, giving her a look of surprise.

I take my seat on the stool at my usual table and look toward the window.

"Today," she says, and begins walking across my view of the outside world. Her heels click on the wooden plank floors. "Today you will show me sadness."

I've figured out that she has this way of trying to sound like she's French or something by speaking English in sentences that sound incomplete. But her profile on the school website says she's from Toledo, Ohio.

Now she's parading before the windows so we can see her skinny figure.

"Today you will show me pain. You will show me fear." She turns quickly to face the class. "But not some dime-store representation of pain! Not some greeting-card image of sadness! Not some matinee horror-movie fear!"

She turns away and gazes out the windows. She speaks again with her back to the class. "You will show me something real. Something terrible. Something you fear will destroy you."

Around me my classmates are rolling their eyes and exchanging glances demonstrating how ridiculous they think the assignment—and the teacher—are. But I'm looking past Miss Numero Uno, through the windows.

"You will do this on newsprint with the oil pastel. You will begin this as I stare out the windows and consider my own demons."

The room falls silent in the absence of her instructions.

Then it's filled with the sounds of pastel on paper as everyone gets to work.

Everyone except me. I sit and stare at the big sheet of newsprint and the little tray of broken oil pastels.

I'm thinking of how the year isn't going how it was supposed to go. I'm thinking of making a list in my tiny journal of things I can't control, but I'm thinking I don't want to think of them at all.

Then I remember I threw my tiny journal into the garbage at the hospital. It failed me. It will never work again.

I'm still staring at the newsprint when Miss Numero Uno finally turns from the windows ten minutes later. I pick up a black pastel and begin working quickly as she slowly moves among the tables.

"Frankenstein? Are you serious?"

Her heels click rapidly on the floor, then stop. "What is this? Adolescent heartbreak? If I wished to vomit I would ride the Ferris wheel!"

Miss Numero Uno works up a sweat storming around the room, shaking her head and delivering scathing critiques.

Finally she stands beside my table. I glance up to her face. She looks surprised, but then I realize it's only her drawn-on eyebrows.

"I am surprised," she says. I guess she really *was* surprised. "I did not think you had it in you."

I look down at my drawing. It's a hastily rendered sketch of a bald little girl with an intravenous fluids bag, labeled with a skull and crossbones, dripping into a hole in her chest. The drawing looks angry, as if I did it to demonstrate how mad I am at the universe. Suddenly I realize I'm breathing hard, like I was fighting a beast instead of drawing a picture. It feels good to have fought the beast. This is what it's all about.

Miss Numero Uno bends lower.

"I know about your sister," she whispers. She sounds almost sad. "I follow your father on the Facebook."

She draws away and walks toward the windows again, where all her serious musings occur.

"Today, only one of my students was able to express

the darkness that threatens to consume her!" She points to me with a dramatic arm, from her shoulder to her fingertip, so that everyone will know I'm the girl about to be consumed by darkness.

Great.

"Honor and distinction to the work of El!" she says dramatically.

As if on cue, the light on the ceiling above me flickers and goes out.

❁ ❁ ❁

Later we're having dinner, the four of us. *All for one, all four one.* We're having brussels sprouts and pomegranate seeds, and tofu laced with turmeric spice. It's typical of the disgusting meals we've been having where everything either supposedly fights cancer or builds Echo's blood cells, which the chemo is destroying.

Echo actually *likes* brussels sprouts, but they make me gag. I remind myself not to complain. *All for one, all four one.* Even though Echo is the only person getting chemo and she actually likes brussels sprouts, so it would make perfect sense if she got to eat all of them and I was spared the nausea. Dad can't get enough of the tofu, but I think it's pretty much been ruined by the turmeric. In a perfect system I'd get the pome-granate seeds, Echo would get the brussels sprouts, Dad the tofu ruined with turmeric, and Mom could just eat the leftovers or something.

I'm trying to choke down one of the aforementioned brussels sprouts when Echo, out of nowhere, pulls a tuft of hair from her head. She has bald spots every-where, shining in the lamplight.

"Look!" she says.

I turn away. "Mom! Could you make her stop?"

"It's like cotton candy," Echo says. I can tell she's pulling more from her head, but I'm not gonna watch.

"Echo, please don't do that at the table," Mom says, sounding a little choked up. "We don't want to acci-dentally get hair in our food."

"She should wear a hairnet or something, like the cafeteria ladies." As soon as I say it I feel terrible.

Dad clears his throat. He doesn't say anything.

But Mom does. "Echo, maybe after dinner we could shave your head like we were talking about."

I give Mom a horrified look.

"The pixie haircut was a good look for you," Mom says. It's been eight days since Mom's stylist cut it short. It looked cute at first, but now it just looks sad. "A nice transition," Mom continues. "But I think the pixie is ready to say good-bye."

Echo puts her face in her palms. "Ugh! I don't wanna be bald."

Dad wipes his mouth with a napkin. "Think of it as your hair going on holiday. A few months of rest."

"A sabbatical," Mom offers.

"A hiatus," says Dad.

I glare at them. "She doesn't know what any of that means!"

"Yes I do, El!"

"Unlike *my* hair," Dad says, putting his hand to his thinning scalp, "when *your* hair goes, it has a round-trip ticket. It'll be back after you're done with chemotherapy."

Echo scowls. "Okay."

"What? Just like that?" I hear myself say it, and I don't know why. I don't know why it matters to me so much.

"Shave it!" Echo shouts, wearing her crazy face. "Shave it off! It looks terrible!"

I look to Mom. "Why don't we just let it fall out on its own? Maybe if she doesn't pull it then it won't come out so fast."

"Echo is being very brave," Mom says. "Let's support her decision to go forward with shaving her head."

Maybe I think she ought to put up more of a fight

about losing her hair. I guess it's a fight she can't win, but at least she could act more upset.

After dinner, after homework and stories, Echo goes into the bathroom with Mom. I need to pee but I have to wait for Echo to do her mouth care. I stand in the hallway waiting my turn, and then I hear the click of a switch and the hum of the hair trimmers.

I turn away and go into our bedroom. I don't get up on my bunk, but stand there waiting, listening. I hear the buzzing, and the sounds of their voices, Mom and Echo, bouncing off all the ceramics of the tile and the tub and the sink and the toilet bowl. It's another opportunity for them to bond and get closer while I'm left on the outside.

I bite my nails. Then I turn to the mirror hung over the desk Echo and I share, see myself looking horrified, and look away. The voices in the bathroom don't sound sad, but my whole body is tense. I peek out the door through the hall and into the living room, where Dad is pretending to be interested in a book.

Finally the buzzing stops. I hear the sink faucet, and the toilet flushing. Echo laughs. "I wanna show El!"

I back into the bedroom to get away.

The bathroom door opens.

"Ta-da!" she shouts. I hear her little feet pound the

floorboards as she runs into the living room.

"Cute!" Dad says.

"Feel my head! It's smooth!"

There's a brief pause.

"Ooh," Dad coos. "That is *so* smooth. You wear it well."

"Where's El?" Echo's footsteps turn my way.

I take another step back.

"El!" she shrieks, entering the bedroom, standing before me. "I'm bald!"

Her expressive face looks even more expressive without hair. Her crazy face is crazier, her funny face is funnier. And her pretty face makes her look like a little glamour model.

"Feel it!" she shouts. "It's smooth!"

She pushes her head against me. Looking down at the pale skin, there are dark bits of stubble and areas that are completely bare. I touch it, and it's waxy like an apple from the grocery.

"I'm bald!" she repeats.

"I see," I say.

"Is it cute?"

"Yes."

"I don't wanna be bald!" She says it with her trademark exasperated voice.

"Don't worry," I say. "It'll grow back."

"I *know* it'll grow back. I want a drink of water!" She runs from the room and I hear her footsteps beat a path to the kitchen, and the refrigerator opening.

Mom stands in the doorway of our bedroom. Her eyes are teary, but she's smiling. She gives me a thumbs-up.

"That's it?" I ask.

"She took it well."

Echo runs back into the room. "Turn off the light! I'm tired!" She falls onto the bed. "I'm tired of being bald!"

She laughs and climbs under the covers.

I turn off the light and shut the door behind me. I stand in the hall. I'm tired, so I don't want to go into the living room. But I don't want to go into the bathroom to brush my teeth, because I don't want to see Mom sweeping up Echo's hair. And I can't go to sleep because I don't want to go into our bedroom, where I imagine Echo's head is shining like the moon.

8

THE NEXT DAY Octavius sits with me at lunch. I don't invite him to, and he doesn't ask. He just sits across from me, and as soon as he does I realize how much I was hoping he would.

"Hey," he says.

"Hey."

"What's for lunch?"

I show him the crust of my sandwich and the container of pomegranate seeds.

"You win," he says.

I look at the four compartments of grayish food on his tray. "I guess so."

"So," he begins, "I made you something."

I don't smile, because I don't want him to know how exciting this sounds to me. "Really? What is it?"

He leans toward me. "Really everyone in your family can enjoy it."

"Let the enjoying begin," I say.

"I need your phone number."

I lean away from him and fold my arms. "Why?"

"So I can text it to you. It's a playlist. A music file of a sampler I made. A bunch of songs to rally your family to kick cancer's butt."

My arms fall to my sides. This sucks. Instead of something just for me, for El, it's something for El, *sister of the girl with cancer.* And everyone else in the family. I try to manage a smile, but I can't feel it. The corners of my mouth cannot turn up.

Just then Sydney—the mean girl who sits to my left in Mr. D's class—walks by, staring at me like I'm some kind of freak. Worse, she's staring at me as I'm looking supremely disappointed.

"What?" I blurt at her.

"Nothing!" she fires back.

"Stop staring at me!"

She stops before me, eyebrows raised in protest. "I'm not!"

I see my hand reach for the crust of my sandwich. My hand disappears behind my field of vision, briefly, and reappears as the crust is flung in the direction of Sydney. By *my* hand. It bounces off her forehead, leaving a small spot of almond butter and blackberry jam where it hits, and falls to the tray of food in her hands.

There's a moment of calm. The sounds of conversation from other tables prevail.

Sydney slowly looks down at the crust of sandwich on her tray, then up at me. Her eyes hold a glossy fury.

"You did *not!*" she seethes.

I briefly consider telling her that apparently I actually *did*. But instead I just watch as she sets her tray down, takes hold of her spoon, and uses it to fling a quantity of mashed potatoes at me. But my view of the mashed potatoes traveling toward me—in a glob, which tumbles end-over-end as it flies through the air—is obscured by the figure of Octavius, who stands and takes the hit for me. In the eye.

"Whoops," Sydney says.

"Ouch," Octavius answers, scooping the potatoes from his eye. "That's kinda warm."

She picks up her tray and storms away.

Then I turn to Octavius. His eyes are big. One eyebrow has mashed potato in it like he's been trudging through a blizzard. I point to it and he wipes it off with his napkin.

"What was *that* about?" he asks.

"Nothing," I answer. "She just despises me. She always looks at me like she hates me. She complains whenever Mr. D thinks I've done something well."

Octavius stares at me like he thinks I've got it all wrong. He opens his mouth like he's gonna tell me as much, but he doesn't say anything.

"What?" I ask.

He smiles, just a little. "Your phone number. So I can text you the playlist."

I roll my eyes, but I don't really mean it. Then I give him my digits, because it's good that I have a friend who will take a hit of mashed potatoes in the eye for me. And it's good to have a friend who already knows how miserable my life is, so there's no need to explain.

The next day, Echo receives exactly twenty-three hats, bandannas, wigs, and turbans by delivery, thanks to Dad posting a picture of her bald head on Facebook with the caption *I wish I could lose my hair so gracefully.* Echo is weirded out by all of it, the hats and wigs, and doesn't take to them so well.

After school, I'm looking at the recent arrivals. "This wig is cute!" I say, holding one of them up.

Echo frowns. "It's blue! If I wear it people will wanna eat me!"

"Echo, nobody is going to eat you."

She gives me a fake disappointed look. "Why not? I'm delicious!"

Mom appears in the doorway of our bedroom. "She's got plenty to choose from if she ever feels like wearing one. And we do want her to wear something on her head whenever she's out in the sun."

"I'm never out in the sun!" Echo shouts. She's not really mad, but she means what she says. "I'm just stuck in here!"

Mom looks at the clock on the wall. "How about a walk, all three of us? It's nice out. And if we stay in the neighborhood where the sidewalks aren't so crowded you won't have to wear a mask."

"Why can't we make all the people at the library go away so I can go there and not wear a mask?"

Echo hates wearing the masks. They keep her from breathing in germs, but she thinks the dinosaurs printed on them make her look like a baby.

Mom picks up Echo's boots. "Put these on, and maybe a sweater. And we should do a hat since it's still sunny on the street."

"Ugh!" Echo pulls the knitted hat over her eyes.

When we finally get down to the sidewalk, the shadows are long. It's still beautiful outside, and Echo is happy to be out. She's wearing the knitted cap with a monkey on it, and when we pass people on the sidewalk, walking their dogs or heading home from work, I look at their eyes to see if they notice there's something wrong with her. With the cap on, all we get are smiles.

Before we even reach the corner, we pass a man who coughs. He sounds really snotty. This makes Mom stop cold in her tracks.

"All right. There are lots of people out on the sidewalks. We should do the mask just to be safe."

"I hate the mask!"

Mom reaches into her bag. "I was on the Centers for Disease Control website, and it says that flu season has already begun. We can't take the chance."

Echo scowls. "This is the worst day ever!"

"Mom, she hates the mask!"

Mom shoots me an angry look. "She's already been to the ER twice since she got out of the hospital. Do you want her to go back to the ER and spend the night? I sure don't want to." She adds a cuss word that she only says when she's really mad.

Mom straps the mask over Echo's mouth and nose. Echo hangs her head.

"I know you don't like it. None of us like it." We begin heading toward the corner, and Mom has a new uprightness in her walk that seems fake. "But this is our new reality."

"It isn't gonna be like this *forever*," I say.

"Right. It's our new, temporary reality." We arrive at the corner. "And since it is our new, *temporary* reality, why don't we stop by the bank and the bodega? We still have lives to live. We still have errands to run. I have a check to deposit, and then we could get some ice cream for after dinner."

"Ice cream!" Echo shouts through her mask.

The bank is another block away, and we have to walk quickly to get there before it closes. We pass through the glass doors and are met by a security guard, tall and beefy.

"Sorry, there's no masks allowed. You'll have to remove it."

Mom looks from the guard to Echo, and back to the guard.

"What?"

"He can't wear a mask. Security reasons." He gestures through the lobby behind him to the bank beyond. "This is a bank."

"She's a *girl*. And I *know* it's a bank. I've been banking here since I was *her* age." She gestures to me.

The security man hooks his thumbs in his belt, which has a gun and other serious-looking things attached to it. "Sorry, ma'am. The mask has to go or *he* has to go."

"Are you kidding me? She's *six*. And her immune system is suppressed from undergoing chemotherapy because she has *cancer*." At the last word, Mom's voice cracks, and she goes from looking like the beautiful, strong mom I've always known—the mom who could always make everything okay—to the mom who could be undone by a security guard saying something that doesn't make sense.

"I'm sorry, ma'am, but evil takes on many disguises."

At this, I can't help but crack a smile. I look to Mom, who's trembling with anger.

"He thinks I'm a bandit!" Echo says through her mask. "Stick 'em up!" she shouts with glee.

But Echo is the only one laughing. Mom's hands shake as she removes Echo's mask, muttering to herself. When she's finished and stuffed the mask away in her coat pocket, the security guard shifts his weight from one foot to another.

"You know what, it's fine. She can wear the mask." He looks embarrassed. "I'm sorry for the trouble."

Mom stares at him for a second. Then her expression softens. "Thank you." She retrieves the mask from her pocket and puts it back on Echo. Then she takes Echo by the hand and leads her through the lobby and into the bank. I follow close behind.

At the teller window, there's a glass jar with a picture of Echo on it, smiling. The teller, a young woman, is also smiling.

"Hello, Grace! Hello, girls!" Her eyes are misty.

Mom says hello. I smile. Echo looks at her own face on the jar. There are jars with Echo's picture at every teller window, about a dozen of them.

"Thank you guys. For doing this." Mom taps the jar with a fingertip.

"It's nothing." The woman hands Mom a receipt for her deposit. "If you don't object, we'll deposit it to your account every Friday at closing."

"That's fine. That's wonderful. *Thank* you."

Mom wipes away a tear. The woman behind the teller window wipes away a tear. But they're both smiling. And the security guard even bows to us like we're royalty and opens the door on our way out.

It's our favorite cancer story so far, and it's our favorite even though it started out as a *bad* story. It's a terrible story that turned out great, and it teaches me that we can still laugh, we can still smile. It makes me think that maybe there'll be more bad stories that end this happily.

When we stop at the bodega for ice cream, they have a jar for Echo, too. The owner says he's counting all the donations and letting us spend the donated amount at the store. There's already a few hundred dollars of credit, so we walk away holding ice creams with Mom not having to open her purse. The ice cream keeps us happy all the way home.

After dinner, Dad and I go to the grocery. It's a long walk to Food Fight, but it's pretty much the only decent-size grocery in this part of Manhattan. The aisles aren't as cramped as the bodegas, or stacked as ridiculously high, and it's more cheerful. I was more than happy to accompany Dad when he asked, especially to get away from the apartment and everything sad that creeps into my head when I'm there.

"Here," Dad says as we enter, and tears off the lower half of a shopping list. "You're good at picking the produce. Whoever gets done first finds the other, okay?"

I take the list from him and smile. "Got it." We each grab a basket and part ways.

The list is even more produce-heavy since Echo's diagnosis. Everything has to be organic, everything has to fight cancer or prevent it, or help build blood cells.

I head to the produce area and look down at the list. I don't think about cancer while picking out organic rainbow chard and organic cauliflower and organic brussels sprouts and organic mangoes and organic cherries. And parsley, also organic. And if I did think about cancer I'd be thinking how it was gonna get its butt kicked by such a colorful basket of organic produce.

"*El,*" says a familiar voice. "Are you okay?"

Standing in front of me, holding a bag of apples, is Mr. D, my English teacher. He's wearing a gray sweatshirt that says *Some College.*

"*Huh?*" I ask.

"You were talking about kicking somebody's butt." He smiles.

"I was?"

"If I heard right. You were kind of muttering."

"Hello," I say, because I'd forgotten to. "Are those apples organic?"

Mr. D looks at the label. "Yes. Or so it says."

"Can you hand me a bag?"

He gives me the bag he's holding and grabs another for himself.

"Thank you."

"No problem." He drops the bag into his cart. "Listen, I've been meaning to talk to you."

"Oh."

"But it seems you've been trying to avoid talking to me." He puts his hands on the cart, then takes them away and puts them behind his back. "The first day of school you seemed so eager to learn, and—"

"I've been getting good marks."

He nods slowly, then begins again. "Yes, your work has been good. *More* than good. But I've been worried you haven't seemed happy. Are you having a hard time adjusting to a new—"

"My sister has cancer." I just blurt it out. "It's called rhabdomyosarcoma. Only five kids in a million get it. So she's lost her hair and she'll lose some of her teeth and who knows what her face will look like. And she has to get chemo every Thursday, and three times a day she has to do this mouth care that makes her throw up sometimes, and on weekends she has to take this gross-tasting medicine twice a day, and she can't go to school."

His face looks stricken. "I'm so sorry."

"And she's only six."

He takes a deep breath, like he'd forgotten to.

"And she hardly ever complains, but I know it's hard for her."

"I'm sure."

"So that's why I keep my head down in class, and why I haven't made any friends, and why the girl you saw on the first day of school is not the girl you've seen every day since."

"I understand. I understand completely. Look,

125

maybe you'd benefit from seeing the school psy—"

"Her name is Echo. And she has cancer. And it isn't fair."

"No, it isn't," he says.

Then we stand there looking at each other. After a few seconds of trying not to cry, a big hot tear rolls down my cheek.

"Can I have a hug?" I ask, my voice cracking. "I need to be picked up. Figuratively speaking."

He doesn't answer right away, and I know it's because it's weird for a guy teacher to be hugging girls from his class in the produce section of Food Fight.

"It's okay," I say. "I shouldn't have asked. Anyway, it was cancer's butt I was muttering about kicking."

He opens his arms to me.

I set down my basket and move in for it. He smells like his aftershave, and also the way Dad smells at the end of the day. After a few more seconds I want to pull away from him, but I don't want him to see my face. Finally I do anyway.

"Sorry," I say.

"No need to be sorry." His sweatshirt is stained with my tears.

"*Hello*," says Dad, who has just appeared. The tone of his voice is one of curiosity.

Mr. D steps toward Dad with his hand extended.

"Are you El's father? I'm Mr. Dewfuss, her English teacher."

"Ah, I've heard good things about you." They shake hands.

"El was just telling me why she's not been feeling like herself. About how upset she is about her little sister."

Dad looks to me.

"I *have* been," I say.

"I didn't say you hadn't," Dad says. "I just—"

"But I feel like you've forgotten about me. I know Echo has cancer and it's toughest on her, but it's tough on me, too."

"I know, honey." With the sad expression on his face he looks suddenly beaten down. "It's tough on all of us."

"Can I have a hug?" My voice cracks again.

Dad smiles and puts down his basket. He welcomes me into his arms.

My cheek against his shoulder, I close my eyes to shut out the fluorescent light. I smell oranges and Dad's deodorant. I hear the whistling of the produce man as he stacks plums.

"It was nice meeting you," says Mr. D, and rolls his cart away. I'd momentarily forgotten he'd been standing there.

"You too," Dad answers.

I draw away from Dad. I see the teary stain I've left on *his* shoulder.

"Feel better?" he asks.

I nod and pick up my basket of produce. "Next time I cry over Echo it's gonna be her college graduation."

He smiles. "I like the way you're thinking."

"Or her wedding. Because she's gonna have a long, happy life."

He reaches for my hand and we walk toward the checkout.

While Dad and I were at Food Fight, someone on the second floor of our apartment brought us homemade daal. It's an Indian lentil meal that smells heavenly, but since we already ate dinner, we're going to have it tomorrow night. Mom lets me have a small bowl of it for a snack while I'm doing my homework.

After brushing my teeth I slip into the bedroom. I leave the door open just a little so the light from the fixture in the short hall can find its way in.

I make my way over to our bunk bed and look at Echo. She's there on the lower half, sleeping, her bald head glowing like the moon. I pull the kitten quilt up to her shoulders. Echo rolls over onto her other side so she is now facing me. She mumbles something in her sleep, and I wonder what thought is behind her words.

I reach down and run my hand over her head. I can feel the peach fuzz. I think of how she likes to show me that smoothing the sides down with water makes the few stray hairs show up more. *See,* she says. *It's growing back.* But it isn't growing back, and it won't really grow back until the twelve weeks of chemo are over with.

I look at her mouth, where the tumor had once pushed her teeth forward, drastically changing her appearance. The tumor has shrunk, and her face in profile is almost back to normal. Her hair is gone, but at least she got to keep her pretty eyebrows and eyelashes. For the moment, anyway. She's also probably paler. She doesn't get as much sun these days, and her blood isn't as healthy.

I think about the tumor, still there, behind her upper teeth on the roof of her mouth. The chemo has made it retreat, but it's still there, in her flesh and bone.

Be gone, cancer. Leave my little sister alone.

I think this, and look at my bald little sister who doesn't even think of wearing hats unless she's in the sun and Mom and Dad make her. I look at the little girl who talks herself into drinking medicine that tastes so bad it makes her throw up, who gets poked and bled and pumped full of poison that fights the cancer but batters her body. I look at the little girl who somewhere in her mind knows that she's fighting for her life, but hasn't allowed herself to cry.

Echo smiles in her sleep, and I wonder from what happy thought. I bend down and kiss her upper lip, the curtain the cancer hides behind.

"Cancer messed with the wrong girl," I whisper.

9

MONDAY, I SIT at Milky's Malts after school. It's an old-fashioned diner a couple of blocks from the Village Arts Academy.

I'm here to meet Octavius, who told me in class he has some big surprise for me. I'm both excited and terrified. I don't really know what sort of outcome I want from meeting him here, and I'm afraid to wonder about it.

I've ordered my malt already, strawberry with whipped cream and a cherry on top, and paid for it at the counter. I didn't want to wait for him to offer to pay, especially if it meant I would wait and then it didn't happen. So I've got who pays for my malt already figured out, and the server brings it just as he comes through the door.

"Hey!" he says. "Thanks for meeting me!"

"Sure thing." I wipe my palms on my uniform skirt.

He slides into the booth across from me. "You already ordered?"

"Yeah. I hope you don't mind." I pull the cherry from the whipped cream and bite it from the stem. It tastes amazing. It's the first thing I've been able to taste in forever. "I was hungry."

"Ah, I was gonna buy."

I smile, but not too much, and shrug. "Next time."

He nods. "So, I've got something for you."

"Really?" This time it's very hard not to grin.

"Yeah. I hope you don't think it's creepy." He stands his book bag up on the seat next to him and reaches for its zipper.

"I, too, am hoping I don't think it's creepy." *Nice and witty*, I tell myself.

"Okay. Okay. Here it is." He opens the bag with dramatic flair, reaches inside, and pulls out—a hat.

It's a red baseball hat that says *Team Echo* in gold stitching. He looks pleased with himself as he hands it to me, then reaches in the bag for another, which he pulls on his head.

"What do you think?" He looks at me, eyebrows raised with hope.

Disappointment washes over me, drowns me. I

stare at the hat, unseeing. I don't want to look up at him because I don't want him to see my eyes.

"Hold on." I leave the table and hurry down the aisle to the bathroom, then rush inside and bolt the door.

I look at the hat in my hands. It's the stupidest, ugliest thing I've ever seen. There's no way I'm even trying it on. I look at my face in the mirror. I hate myself at this moment, for being such an idiot I'd think he'd get something for me that was really for *me*. But I hate *him* even more. First the "Echo's Fight Song" mix, and now this. He just wants to cozy up to the celebrity sick kid, like everyone else. I was a fool not to see he's only interested in Echo.

I splash water on my face, then dry it with toilet paper because they're out of paper towels. I storm from the bathroom and down the aisle and drop into the booth across from him. I hold up the hat and shake it at him.

"This is the ugliest hat I've ever seen, and giving it to me is completely creepy." I lean across the table, and he draws back in fear. "She's *my* sister, not yours."

He keeps looking from my eyes to my cheek. He looks hurt but also distracted.

"What?" I demand. I'm trembling with rage and every kind of bad feeling.

"Then I guess you don't want to see the Team Echo T-shirts?"

I fling the hat at him, and it bounces off his chest and onto his lap. Then I grab my bag and leave. I slip on a napkin and lose my balance, bumping into another table, spilling an old man's iced tea onto his grilled cheese. The old man raises his voice in protest as I turn away and rush to the exit. The bells on the door jingle angrily as I burst through it, and the cool outside air meets the wet of my eyes.

I stumble down the street, not knowing where I'm going, or where I *should* be going. I reach up to touch my face and peel off the scrap of toilet paper that's apparently been stuck to my cheek since the bathroom.

After dinner, Dad and I walk with Echo to the gelato shop. I'm not so much in the mood for it after the Octavius fiasco, but when Echo feels like eating something, especially something with fat or protein in it, we have to drop what we're doing and make it happen. Chemo makes people lose weight, and Echo was already skinny before cancer.

It's a pretty evening. The leaves on the trees in the sidewalk planters have just begun changing colors.

It occurs to me that I've noticed that the evening is pretty, and I wonder if it means I've gotten used to having a little sister who has cancer. But I feel guilty for thinking it's a pretty evening, because every evening is pretty terrible for Echo. Even if she doesn't realize it.

"I'm gonna get something pink!" she says through her mask. She always chooses by color. "What color are you gonna get, El?"

"I'm thinking I'll get something pistachio-colored."

"Pistachio isn't a color!"

"It is at the paint store."

She furrows her brow; her eyes look kooky. "We aren't going to the paint store!"

"No? Then I'll get something a very light whitish-green."

The gelato shop is narrow, with a long counter and a row of small tables for two across from it. Echo skips back and forth along the counter, looking at the pinks, which include bubble gum, lobster bisque, peppermint, black cherry, birthday cake, and strawberry. I already know I'm sticking with pistachio.

"Can I please have birthday cake?" Echo asks the girl at the counter. "I can't wait for my birthday!"

The counter girl looks at Echo's bald head and germ

mask and can't hide her sadness. She tries to smile, but I know that, like me, she's wondering if Echo will live to see another birthday.

"A single or a double?" she asks.

"A single!" Echo jumps up and down.

"You can have a double if you'd like," Dad says. He never misses an opportunity to try to stuff Echo with more food.

"I'm not hungry enough for two," Echo says.

"And a double of pistachio for me," I add.

"Make that just a single, please," Dad says. "And nothing for me, thanks." He'll spend money to get Echo to eat, but I can only get a single and he can't get anything.

The counter girl smiles grimly and turns away to get our scoops. I gather napkins and a couple of little plastic spoons. The girl returns with our gelato cups.

"Can I have a sample?" Echo asks.

I look to Dad, but he's got the bank app open on his phone, checking to see if we're not too broke from medical expenses to afford two scoops of gelato. He's oblivious.

The girl smiles. "What would you like a sample of?"

"Birthday cake!"

I roll my eyes. "You don't get a sample of the flavor you're already getting."

"It's okay," the girl says. She takes a tiny spoon and dips it into the tub, then returns. "Here you go."

"Thank you!" Echo lifts her mask to taste it. "Mmm. I'm glad I got that flavor."

"That'll be five twenty-five."

Dad reaches for his wallet.

"Let me get that." It's a voice from behind us, a man ten years younger than Dad. He looks to the counter girl. "Please just add it to my order."

The counter girl looks from the stranger to Dad. Dad looks from the girl to the stranger.

"Please," says the man, who wears a sweater-vest over a plaid shirt. "It would make me very happy if you'd let me."

"Thank you," Dad says, managing a smile.

"Thank you," I say.

"You're welcome." The man smiles a kind smile.

I nudge Echo. "Say thank you, Echo."

"Thank you! Thank you!"

The man smiles down at her. "You're very welcome."

We turn from the counter and the generous man. But directly behind him is a face I recognize. It's Sydney, the girl who sits to my left in Mr. D's class. The girl who always groans if I say anything that sounds halfway smart, anything that makes Mr. D happy. My mashed-potato-slinging nemesis. She stares at me

137

with a strange expression, and then at Echo.

"Excuse me," I say, 'cause she's kinda in the way. She steps aside, but stares at us, mouth agape, as we move past.

Wonderful. Now that *she* knows, the whole school will know. That I'm the girl with the sad life, with the sick little sister, who has to eat charity gelato.

Even ice cream has become miserable.

And school is about to get unbearable.

❀ ❀ ❀

The next day at school is the worst ever. I refuse to even look at Octavius, and so I don't say a word to anyone, and nobody says a word to me. But everyone looks at me when I walk past. They look at me like they know something about me I don't want them to know. And I feel like they're whispering, *Ooh, poor girl. Her sister has cancer. She can't have fun because she's too sad.*

On my way home, dogs out for their walks can smell the sadness on me. They hide behind their owners' legs as I go by. When Mom says hello to me on my way in the door, it's the first words spoken to me since she said good-bye as I left in the morning.

In the kitchen I hear my phone vibrate on the counter. I pick it up and see a message from Maisy.

Hey El! I miss you soooooooo much. How r things?

"Things are wonderful," I say to the empty kitchen. I don't text back, then leave the phone on the counter and open the pantry. All the food looks tasteless, but I spot a neglected old friend below the bottom shelf. My tennis racquet. I grab it and a can of balls and storm through the living room, past Mom, and out the door.

Down the stairs and outside, I stand on the front steps and look up and down the block.

"Welcome to the almost-Greenwich-Village Tennis Club," I announce to nobody. I pop the lid off the can and roll the three balls into my hands. Down the steps to the sidewalk, I spin around, looking for a place to hit against. But there are no clean stretches of empty wall. Instead there are windows every few feet, basement windows and steps and iron rails, and window boxes with flowers, not to mention trees in planters and parked cars packed into every possible space on the street.

No matter. I drop a ball onto the sidewalk, and as it comes back up I whack it with my best forehand groundstroke. I manage to hit a brick wall across the street in a space between windows, and it bounces back my way. I meet it in the street and whack it with my backhand. I'm out of practice but you wouldn't know

139

by the force of my swing. The ball hits the door of a town house and bounces back. This time I catch it on the second bounce and whack it with another backhand, into the side of a parked van. I have little time to react to the return but manage a forehand drop shot that lands in the downstairs well of a basement.

I call out the score. "Fifteen-love." A messenger on a bicycle smiles as he rides past. I drop another ball and mash it. This time I miss the wall. It bounces off a first-floor window and comes back through the branches of a small tree in a planter. I whack it back across and it short-hops the wall and goes high. I wait for it, maneuvering with stellar footwork, and meet it with an overhand smash that rips the face off a flower in a window box across the street.

"Thirty-love."

The last ball I drop and smack, but it's way too low and thumps into the side of a fancy car right across the narrow street. The car alarm sounds, bouncing off buildings as the ball rolls down the block. I stand with my arms at my sides for a moment. Then a guy leans out the third-story window of the town house across the street, glaring at me.

"Sorry," I call up.

He points his key at the car and clicks the alarm off, then closes the window and disappears.

I turn to fling my racquet away, but before I can I see my dad, standing at the top of the steps to our apartment. He has his hands in his pockets.

"You miss tennis?"

My shoulders sag. I nod.

He looks around, up and down the block. "It's a nice day for it."

I point across the street with my racquet. "I just killed a flower."

"How was school?" He's acting like I've been playing tennis, not like he's just witnessed me having a tantrum. I decide that's pretty generous of him.

I look him up and down. "Aren't you supposed to be teaching babies to paint? Did you get fired too?"

He shakes his head. "Nope. In-service day at the Academy of Privileged Toddlers. No school."

"Oh."

He sits on the stairs leading up to our apartment, and I join him. He's right about the day, which is a little crisp, but clear. It's a perfect day for tennis if there were a court to play on. I think about what the kids at my old school would be doing on a day like today and decide the girls would be playing tennis in the basement gym. Or basketball.

Dad looks at his cell phone, then nudges me. "You never answered my question."

"School? It was possibly the worst day ever. But I got through it."

He nods. He doesn't try to talk me out of feeling that way about it. I stare the short distance to the town houses across the street, but I can see him out of the corner of my eye.

"Good," he says.

"The girl from Mr. D's class who saw us with Echo at the gelato shop has apparently told the whole school about her cancer. So today everyone stopped talking when I walked past. It's like they held their breath."

"Maybe you're imagining it."

"Or maybe she's told the whole school about me and my sad life. And how a stranger paid for our ice cream because we don't have any money."

"That was very thoughtful of him," Dad says quietly. "Not everyone is gonna understand it."

I'm sure he's come out here because of something unpleasant. Bad news about Echo, or all of us. I'm too accustomed to bad news to worry much about it. I'll just let it come, like I'm buried in sand and the tide is rolling in to drown me.

"Your mom says Maisy has been texting and emailing you for weeks but you've been avoiding her."

"What makes Mom think that?"

"Maisy's mom called her."

I let that sink in. I picture it. "I suppose Mom told Maisy's mom about Echo's cancer?"

"I think there's a very strong possibility that came up."

I frown at the street below.

"Don't you still want to be friends with her?" he asks.

I watch a bird fly frantically past. "It's just . . ." I don't have a complete answer.

"Sometimes I blame myself," Dad says. "Like if I made more money, you guys would see the dentist and the doctor more often. Maybe they'd have caught it sooner."

I wait for more, then glance at him. He's staring through the sidewalk.

"You're a good dad." I put my arm around him. "The best. The cancer grew so fast. That's what the doctor said."

"Thanks for saying that." He puts his arm around me, returning the favor. "Thanks for lifting me up."

"All for one, all four one." I say it without even a trace of sarcasm.

I look up and down the street, at the trees in the planters with their leaves dressing for autumn, the pretty old town houses with fancy ironwork on the steps. The flowers in the window boxes, even though one of them is missing its face thanks to my careless overhand smash. "This really is a lovely place. Manhattan, and the Village. Especially if you like people." I bounce the face of my racquet off my foot. "And I *do* like people. I'm just having a tough time at the moment. It's entirely my fault I don't have any friends."

"Oh, you've got friends," Dad says, and looks back down the block as if expecting someone. He glances again at the phone in his hand, the hand that isn't on my shoulder, then sets it down and wipes a tear away with his palm. I wipe mine away with the arm of my sweater. Tears are too commonplace now to be embarrassing, for either of us.

"So what's the bad news?" I ask.

There's a pause, so I turn to him.

"No bad news," he says.

"Then why do you look sad?"

"I'm sad that you expect bad news."

I lean into him and close my eyes.

It's perfect, just for a moment, just the love between me and Dad. Then there's the sound of someone clearing their throat, and Dad leans away from me. Maisy is standing at the bottom of the steps, holding a single yellow rose, looking at me questioningly, measuring my expression. My hand covers my mouth, but I feel myself rising to my feet.

"Why are you shutting me out?" she asks. "It's not fair."

Dad rises and goes inside our building. I sit back down. "There's a lot of *not fair* going around. Just ask Echo."

Maisy throws the rose onto the sidewalk. Her fists are clenched at her sides. "Being friends isn't supposed to be like that. When you're in pain *I'm* supposed to be in pain. Your fear is supposed to be *my* fear. Otherwise what's the point?"

I stand again. I look down at her, frowning at the bottom of the steps.

"That's what you want? A piece of my misery?"

Her foot stomps, crushing the rose on the sidewalk. "Isn't that what I just *said*?"

Her face falls as I glide down the front steps, until I'm on the sidewalk with her. I look down at the broken yellow rose.

"Hang on." I walk quickly to the town house across the street, to the window box, and find the face of the decapitated flower. It's got a half inch of stem connected to it, and a yellow center with white petals, a few of which are missing. I pick it up and return across the street to Maisy, whose eyes remain directed at the sidewalk. I hold the flower face in my palm, beneath her gaze.

"Here," I say. "Damaged."

Her hand takes it. Broken stem held between her fingers, she twirls it. Then she bends down and retrieves the yellow rose.

"Here," she says. "Crushed."

My hand takes it. I bring it to my nose. It smells like cupcake frosting at Maisy's birthday.

Then we move closer, and our arms go around each other, her familiar hair against my cheek. I return the yellow rose to my nose. I smell it and think that I'll never forget the fragrance of this crushed yellow rose, and how it feels to have my best friend back.

Maisy stays for dinner, so there are no texts from her to ignore while we eat. Instead we sit side by side, and I eat with my left hand so I can hold hers with my right. I answer all of her questions, I tell her how great school hasn't been, how wonderful everything is not. I don't tell her how scared I am about Echo and her cancer—not in this moment—because Echo sits across the table from us.

After dinner the five of us go out for gelato and hot chocolate, and I see that the gelato shop now has a jar with Echo's face on it, and it occurs to me that of course Maisy would know about Echo, with all the jars everywhere in the neighborhood.

During dinner and gelato and the walk between,

I of course hear all about my old school and my old friends, who Maisy assures me aren't *old* friends, but just friends.

I promise her that I'll return her texts, that we'll do this all the time. Me at her house, she at ours, and things that we used to do, strictly for fun. And I mean every word I say.

It's practically the best night ever. It gives me hope.

I hope it's a hope I can hold on to.

10

IN SPITE OF how great the evening was with Maisy, the next day at school I am still most definitely not looking forward to seeing Octavius. During phys ed I'm so distracted I get hit in the face with the volleyball, which does not feel good, and I decide I'll go to the bathroom and hide out through science class. But when I get there, it smells so disgusting I turn around and go to class anyway.

I come in at the last moment and avoid eye contact with Octavius as Mr. Bleeker introduces a lesson about the disappearance of bees. Bleeker especially likes talking about the science of depressing things, which is just what I need in my state of mind. He couldn't possibly have us learn about something that doesn't end with the extinction of mankind or some other species. Today it's the extinction of bees and the resulting elimination of everything colorful and delicious in our diets.

At least there's no lab today, so I won't have to sit with Octavius.

But then as Mr. Bleeker is describing the bland beige foods that will remain in the absence of bees, something hits me in the side of the face and falls to my desk. It's a triangle made of folded paper, with the words *Open, El.*

I know who it's from, and I won't look at him. But I glare with disdain at the triangle of folded paper, then brush it to the floor.

"Crackers will still be in play," says Mr. Bleeker. "Any big fans of saltines here?"

Then I hear the sneaky, slow tear of paper to my left. I swear I can hear Octavius writing, and folding, and then when Mr. Bleeker turns his back to the class it flies at me, hitting the same spot on my left cheek, again falling to my desk.

I ignore it for as long as I can, but then I realize I don't really *want* to ignore it. I look down, pretending to be annoyed, and see the words *Please open* in Octavius's handwriting.

I sigh, then begin unfolding it.

If you want the truth, meet me at Frenchy's Coffee after school.

I don't answer. I'm not sure I want the truth or anything at all from Octavius.

All through art class I'm not sure whether I'll go to meet him. I'm having a hard time weighing the pros and cons because Miss Numero Uno is so strangely cheerful it's frightening. I'm not sure as I draw our apartment building from memory, which is today's assignment, and I'm still not sure when the bell rings and I hurriedly finish my illustration, then pack up my book bag and wander outside into the gray day.

I'm not sure as I drift down the sidewalk, and I'm not sure even as I push through the door at Frenchy's Coffee and spot Octavius sitting at a table in the corner behind a giant whipped drink.

He gives a little wave and I turn to the counter, where the guy in the apron is waiting for me.

"What will you have?" he asks in a French accent. I'm thinking this must be Frenchy.

I look up at the menu, but it's just words. Ordinarily I would order a delicious, creamy drink with whipped cream like the one Octavius is hiding behind. But I need to order something that shows Octavius how mad I am at him. "Something dark," I finally say. "I want the exact opposite of what *he's* having." I gesture toward Octavius.

Frenchy raises an eyebrow. I think he's possibly pleased with my decision. "I think you will enjoy the Turkish coffee. It is the perfect drink to disagree with his frothy concoction." He tilts his head toward Octavius.

"Perfect," I reply. Frenchy rings me up and I play off my actual shock at how much this Turkish coffee costs. It must be coming all the way from Turkey.

Having ordered and paid, I'm left with little choice but to join Octavius. I walk over and drop my book bag beside his. Our book bags can sort it out while he and I do the same.

"Thanks for coming," he says.

I fall into the chair opposite him. I don't want to say *sure*, because I wasn't and I'm still not, and *you're welcome* sounds more generous than I'm feeling. So I say nothing.

He touches the straw in his drink. "I'm sorry I've been less than completely forthcoming. I understand why you'd think it's creepy for me to take such an interest in Echo."

I watch him and wait for more. He looks across the coffeehouse, then back to me.

"I didn't want to tell you my story, or all of it, because I know how important it is to stay positive when you love someone who's fighting cancer."

He looks down and addresses his hands, folded on the table.

"My mother isn't a doctor."

I allow myself to feel this. And it doesn't feel horrible. Maybe he's embarrassed because his mom has some terrible job that isn't prestigious. The Village Arts Academy can do that to kids.

But then it hits me.

"If your mom isn't a doctor, how do you know so much about Midtown Children's Hospital?"

"My sister," he begins, and pauses as Frenchy sets down a giant, wide mug of black coffee with tan foam on top. There are two tiny shortbread cookies on the saucer.

"What is that?" Octavius asks, nodding at my drink.

"It's a Turkish coffee. I've been drinking these my whole life." I allow myself a lie. I owed him one. I raise the mug to my lips and take a sip. It tastes terrible, and I fight back whipping my head and grimacing.

Octavius takes a pull on his delicious-looking whipped drink and wipes his mouth. Then he takes a big breath and lets it out. "My sister had cancer."

"Oh," I reply, instantly feeling like an insensitive jerk. "How is she doing?"

Octavius suddenly looks very small. He takes another pull on his frozen blended drink. "This is why you shouldn't be talking to me. Because you need to hear only positive stories. Happy endings. You need to believe that everything's going to turn out okay." He looks to the door and back to me. "Because it *is* going to turn out okay."

My eyes have gotten large, but the room is out of focus.

"But it didn't," I say. It falls from my mouth lifelessly. *"Did* it?"

He shakes his head. Then he lowers his face and puts his hand over his eyes.

All at once I feel it, like it happened to me, like it was *my* sister and not his. I feel what empathy feels like, and realize that I have never felt it before. I knew what it meant, and thought I had felt it, but I never had.

I feel it now.

"What was her name?"

He answers without showing his eyes. "Cassia."

"Cassia," I repeat. "What a pretty name."

He takes his hand away from his face, revealing

the grief. "She was eight when she died." He stares into space, drums the table with his fingers. "But she fought so hard. And she lived like she meant it."

I've never seen so much of a human before as Octavius at this moment. "I'm sure she did."

"She loved opera. And ice cream."

"What was her favorite kind?"

"Birthday cake." He smiles. "And she was crazy about kites. She loved flying them at the park, and at the beach. She could build them herself! There's one that she made hanging in her room."

"I'd like to see it."

"The kite? Or her room?"

"All of it."

Octavius smiles again.

"And she loved making sandcastles at the shore. She wanted to live through to summer so she could have her toes in the sand again."

"Did she?"

"No."

I don't even know what to say to this. I don't know how the universe can be so cruel.

"But she was stage four," he adds quickly. "She had much worse odds." He looks intently at me. "You said Echo was stage one, right? Everything's gonna work out for her." He sits against the chairback, then shakes his head. "I've felt like I'm betraying Cassia by taking an interest in Echo. Like since Cassia lost her fight, now I'm trying to be on the side of a kid with a better chance than she had. Like I'm one of those kids who cheers for the best team so they never have to lose. But my dad taught me that you cheer for the home team, and if the home team isn't playing you cheer for the underdog."

"Sounds like *my* dad," I say.

Octavius looks away, then takes another drink. "I'm sorry. I shouldn't be dumping this on you. It's enough for you to have to go through what you're going through with Echo."

I wipe my eyes on my forearm and take a sip of my Turkish coffee. It tastes richly bitter, like centuries of suffering.

"It sounds like you're going through it too," I say. "With Cassia. *And* with Echo." I take another sip of the coffee. "My dad might say that our favorite team is Echo, and our second-favorite team is whoever is playing against cancer today." My eyes feel shiny. "And if you believe that, if you feel the same way as my dad, then I say *welcome aboard.* There's room for you in the bleachers."

He smiles, then laughs a little.

I take another sip of the coffee.

It hits me.

"I taste this!" I practically shout. I look to Frenchy at the counter. He smiles as I give him the thumbs-up. Then I look back to Octavius. "I *feel* this." It's a strange revelation. I put my hand to my heart and feel it beating. "I feel *all* of this."

❈ ❈ ❈

Late at night I'm lying in bed, looking at the stars painted in fluorescent white on the ceiling above me. Echo is beneath me on the lower bunk. The classical station plays at low volume in the darkness, the music we sleep to. The music gets quiet, and I'm able to hear my parents talking in the living room.

"Something has to give."

Dad says that, then the song occupies the quiet space again.

I listen, but all I can hear is a string section.

". . . just way beyond our ability," Mom says as the strings screech to a halt.

I sit up, then climb down the ladder to the floor. I walk the wood floors quietly in my socks and pajamas and put my ear to the door. I wait for a moment but hear nothing from the living room. I can picture them staring into space, trying to see their way through an impossible obstacle. Then I open the door to find exactly that. They look up from their distances to me standing in the short hallway.

"Back to bed, El," Dad says.

I don't move right away.

"Is everything okay?" Mom asks.

"I can't sleep." I observe that Mom is holding a can of beer. Dad has a plate of toast in front of him. "I drank Turkish coffee after school."

Dad smiles. "Well, then you should probably stay up all night writing a tragedy."

"I could write *our* story," I say glumly.

"You could write our story if you like," Mom says. "But it doesn't have to be seen as a tragedy."

I'm still standing between the bedroom door and the living room. "What were you guys talking about?"

Dad looks to Mom, which means he's being careful not to say anything she doesn't approve of.

Mom sighs. "Just . . . tough choices."

Meowzers passes beneath me, rubbing against my shins. "Are we gonna have to leave Manhattan and move someplace cheaper?"

Dad uncrosses his legs and reaches for his toast. "There are worse things than—"

"Nobody said anything about moving," Mom cuts in. Dad smiles and takes a bite of toast.

"Am I gonna have to go back to my old school?"

Dad speaks through his toast. "There are worse things than that."

Mom gives him a look. "Nobody said anything about you having to leave your school."

Meowzers does another pass against my legs. I look down but don't pick him up. I'm thinking it's weird that I'm worried I'd leave a school I thought I was miserable at. "We need some kind of miracle, don't we?" I hear myself say.

Mom sighs again. "Waiting for miracles is not the best way to approach life's difficulties." She takes a sip of beer. "But a miracle would be nice."

Dad speaks through his toast. "A miracle would be most welcome."

11

THE NEXT MORNING I wake up and hang my head to look at the bunk below. I've gotten in the habit of doing this—staring at Echo's form to see if she's breathing. She's not really in imminent danger, but I find myself doing it anyway. But she isn't there.

I climb down the ladder from my bunk and walk out into the hall. Mom and Dad look up from the kitchen table. I smile, just for them, then take two steps to the bathroom door. I can hear Echo in there.

I have to pee, but the door is locked. I wait.

I hear the toilet flush, then the sink faucet running. Both these sounds make me need to pee even worse.

"Echo!"

"Give her a minute," Mom calls from the table.

I hear Echo brushing her teeth. Then the sound of her spitting.

I keep waiting.

"What are you *doing*?"

"I have to do my mouth care!" she shouts through the door.

I groan. I'm ready to pee into a bucket. Or Meowzers's litter box.

I put my ear to the door. I hear the sound of her swishing something in her mouth, then spitting, and the clink of a cup being placed on the sink. Then her little voice.

"This is hard, but I can do hard things."

I listen carefully. I try to quiet the beating of my heart.

She almost whispers what comes next. "One, two, three, *go*."

There's quiet, then she makes a gagging noise, and I hear her set the cup down.

Then the door opens, and her expressive face is painted with sadness. Her head hangs, her arms are limp.

"You did it!" I say. "High five."

I hold out my hand and she slaps it mechanically. She trudges past me into our bedroom and falls onto her bed.

I go into the bathroom and shut the door. As I sit peeing I see a crumpled piece of paper on the floor by the wastebasket. I reach for it, uncrumple it. I smooth it out on the sink counter beside me.

It's a small piece of paper, with a drawing by Echo of a bald little girl with tears dripping from her eyes. The words *Miss you hair* are written across the top.

At this moment I realize she isn't oblivious. She isn't just a happy-go-lucky kid who is too silly to realize she has cancer.

She feels all of it. Every poke, every disgusting taste, every staggering ounce of poison dumped into her port, every fearful thought. She gets it all, she feels it all, she suffers it all, but she's amazingly strong. She knows the size of the beast she's fighting, and she's fighting it with all her might, and every bit of good humor she can manage.

I brush my teeth. I turn on the "Echo's Fight Song" mix made by Octavius, jump in the shower, and wash my hair, which I used to complain about for being too thick. It's the first time I've played the sampler, and it shreds me. There are songs with titles of "Heroes" and "All Right" and "Lust for Life." They all seem to be about a little girl who just wants to have fun, who wants to live, and see her friends, and be queen, and feel all right. Things every little girl should be able to hope for.

It drains my eyes. It fills my heart.

I stay in the shower until the water is no longer warm. Then I dry off and join my parents at the table. There's toast and eggs and tea.

"I've got an idea I want to run by you," Mom says.

"What?" I stir sugar into my Darjeeling.

"So, I've been brainstorming ideas of how to reach people who have a need for a chemo dress or other types of chemo clothes. There're message boards and places I can advertise. But the problem is, the people who might want a dress or a shirt with a port for chemo are people with the same sort of financial stress we are feeling right now."

I take a bite of toast and chew it. I swallow.

"Give them a price range," I say. "Let them pay just your expenses if that's all they can pay, and if they are able to afford the beautiful work of an amazingly talented and semi-famous dressmaker, then let them pay a higher amount."

Mom smiles and looks to Dad. "Did we raise El this way? Is she this good a person because of anything we've done?"

Dad smiles. "Probably not."

Mom laughs and leans over to kiss my cheek.

"I'm not such a good person," I say.

They look to me quizzically, so I lay Echo's drawing out for them to see. Dad shakes his head; Mom puts her hand to her heart.

"I thought she was oblivious until I saw this." I look toward the hall to make sure she isn't coming. "I seriously thought she was taking everything so well because she was too young and clueless to notice what she was going through. But she's *strong*."

"You're right, she is strong." Mom puts her hand on mine. "This is a new experience for all of us, El."

"You're strong, too." Dad fills my glass with grape-fruit juice. "You're doing so well."

❁ ❁ ❁

After school, Octavius is quiet as we ride the train up to his neighborhood in Hamilton Heights. He's quiet on the birdless sidewalks where the shadows grow long. He's quiet leading me into his building and up three flights of stairs, while keying us into the apartment, and past his mother, who looks up from the kitchen table and says nothing.

We walk down a short hall to a closed door. Octavius looks at me, then turns the knob.

"El, meet Cassia."

"Cassia," I hear myself say as the door swings open and her world is revealed. It's exactly as she left it when her lifeless body was carried out two years earlier. I step inside.

There are shelves filled with books, and mobiles hanging from the ceiling of dozens of tiny paper kites in bright colors, and of the winged horse Pegasus. And clouds and strings of raindrops and autumn leaves, and a rainbow painted across the wall. There is a window with a view of someone else's window across an alley.

There is a record player and a stack of records, all of them opera. I pick up one whose cover shows a plump, shiny-faced woman in an evening gown singing to the lights.

"That was her favorite," Octavius says. I put it back on the stack. "It's on the turntable. Check it out." He clicks a switch, lifts the needle, and sets it down. The crackling dissipates as the needle finds the groove, and a soprano voice—singing in Italian—swells and fills the room. It's beautiful, and mournful, and so different from everything I see in the room, like it's the missing ingredient of what a human can feel. Like it's the sound of Cassia crying.

Above her bed is a string, like a clothesline, with get-well cards draped from it. Also hanging from the ceiling, in a corner, is a yellow paper kite with the words *Look out below!* painted in cursive. The tail is adorned with dozens of paper identification bracelets from the chemo clinic.

On the walls there are posters of puppies and photos of family, and drawings that would make me smile if I could smile.

There's also a calendar with drawings rendered in a style I recognize as being that of Octavius. It shows chemo every day except Sunday, when it shows *Ice cream and carousel!* instead. There are drawings of sundaes and ice-cream cones and painted ponies on the Sundays, and hypodermic needles and pills and hospital buildings on the other days.

Lying on her pillow is a photo of Cassia, before she got sick, smiling with bright eyes and teeth and thick black hair. I pick it up and study it closely.

"She's beautiful."

Then I lean in close to see something written in cursive marker on the wall beside her bed.

This is hard, but I can do hard things.

My knees buckle. The photograph falls from my hand.

I turn away from the writing, put my hand on the desk to steady myself.

Octavius reaches for my shoulder. "You okay?"

"I heard Echo say those same words."

He nods, puts the photograph back on the pillow. "They teach it at the clinic. One of the better rallying cries." He's studying my eyes, but I'm not gonna come apart in front of him.

I take a deep breath. "Can I come back and visit sometimes?" I ask.

Octavius looks puzzled. "Do you mean me, or—"

"Cassia," I say. "And you." I take a look around the room, then nod. "I really need for you to be on Echo's team."

12

TWO DAYS LATER I'm walking home after school, accompanied by Octavius. I've finally agreed to let him meet Echo. I'm worried that she'll think it's weird that he wants to meet her, but I feel like I need to let him since he let me meet Cassia, even though it's way different since Echo is alive and Cassia isn't.

"Please don't bring up Cassia," I say as we walk down my block.

"I won't."

"And let's just make it casual, like you're over to do homework with me, and she just happens to be there."

"Okay."

"And don't bring up her cancer, or talk about it, unless she does."

"Got it."

We arrive at our front steps, and I turn to him. "Just be your charming self. But without the part that knows so much about cancer."

He puts his hand on my shoulder. "Thank you for letting me meet her."

I don't say *you're welcome*, because again I'm not so sure that I feel like he *is* welcome. I punch in the key code and open the front door. Up the stairs we go, and suddenly the image of Echo's body being carried *down* the stairs invades my head. I push it away, out of my brain, as I have become practiced at doing with scary thoughts, and begin whistling "Lust for Life" from the fight song sampler Octavius made for Echo.

We rise to the third-floor landing and our door on the left. I turn my key, open it a crack, and call out, "Mom, I'm here with a friend. Is everyone wearing clothes?"

Mom appears and opens the door the rest of the way. She smiles at me, then Octavius.

"I'm guessing you must be Octavius?"

"That's me."

"I've heard so much about you. I'm Grace, El's mom. Please come in!"

"Thank you."

It's fairly horrifying that she said she's heard any-thing at all about Octavius, like I go around talking about him all the time or something. The place is crowded with her dressmaking stuff, with a dress form mannequin standing in the middle of the living room. Opera plays on the radio. Octavius better not say anything about Cassia liking opera.

"So, me and Octavius were gonna do some homework," I announce to Mom. "And maybe hang out a bit."

"Don't let me stop you," Mom says, a sewing needle between her lips. "But please wash your hands first."

"Are you making a dress?" Octavius asks. I roll my eyes.

"Yes! That's what I do. This one is actually designed to allow easy access to a chemotherapy port. That's so when someone is getting treatment for cancer or some other disease requiring chemotherapy they can feel pretty. Even on the days they have to go to the clinic."

Octavius approaches the dress form. "Wow. That is so cool."

"See?" Mom pushes a flap of fabric aside and tugs on a little zipper. "And then down here, at the hip, a zipper vent for the line to come out of after it's been installed. It's more comfortable this way."

"Cassia never had anything that pretty."

I can't believe Octavius said that. All the coaching

I did and practically the first thing that comes out of his mouth is his experience with cancer. At least Echo wasn't in the room. Mom gives a look like she's interested in hearing more, but she's not gonna be hearing any more from Octavius, as I drag him into the kitchen.

"What was that?" I ask once we've reached the kitchen. I wash my hands at the sink.

He's looking at the *All for one, all four one* chalkboard on the refrigerator. "This is a cool idea."

"Can you please just try to remember what I asked of you?"

He looks to me. "Huh? Oh. Yeah."

"Wash your hands. Have you forgotten *everything*?"

"No." He moves to the sink to wash his hands.

Just then, Echo skips into the kitchen. She stops when she sees Octavius.

"Who are you?" she asks.

Octavius about melts at the sight of her. "I'm Octavius. Who are you?"

"I'm Echo. I'm El's sister. I'm a girl but I'm bald. And I don't get to go to school. I have cancer."

"Nice to meet you, Echo."

"Nice to meet you, Octopus." She thinks she's pretty funny.

"Do you miss school?"

170

"Yeah. I like pretending that Mommy's dress forms are other girls who have to stay home. And we have class together."

Octavius smiles. I'm watching him react to her.

"Is that fun?" he asks.

"Not really. But it's less un-fun than not doing it."

"You crack me up," he says. "Do you like flying kites?"

Echo looks at Octavius like he's crazy. "Of course I do!"

Octavius smiles. "I've got one I'd like to give you. Next time I see you."

"Thank you!" She takes her water bottle from the fridge. "Well, I gotta do homework. My teacher will be here in a little while and she's not happy if it isn't finished."

"Good luck against cancer."

"Good luck with my sister!" She skips away.

I sit at the table. Octavius drops into a chair across from me. He looks like he's waiting for me to say something.

"I don't know why she said that," I say. "The 'good luck with my sister' thing."

Octavius just looks at me but doesn't say anything. So I need to change the subject.

"Are you really gonna give her Cassia's kite?"

Octavius nods. "She'd like that. She built it to fly. Not to decorate her room."

He's so wise. But I don't ever want to be wise the way that Octavius is. I don't want to learn what he's learned. "You did well with Echo," I say.

"Thanks. You did a nice job protecting her."

This brings tears from my eyes. Crying happens so much now, I don't ever wonder why or even try to stop it. "Thanks."

Octavius looks over his shoulder toward the living room. "Should we actually do homework or something?"

I roll my teary eyes. "How about we open our folders, but we can be friends for real while we *pretend* to do homework."

He smiles. "That's even better." He opens a folder, takes a math problem sheet out. "She looks good without hair."

"You think?" I bite a fingernail. "I can't look at her bald head without thinking that it's just an emblem of her having cancer."

He looks at me. He studies my face. "She has your eyes."

"My mom's."

He nods. "I wish . . ."

"What?"

"I regret that I didn't shave my head when Cassia lost her hair."

"Why?"

"To show solidarity. Team Cassia and all that."

I look at his face. I picture him without hair.

"It wouldn't have helped," I conclude. Then I bite a fingernail. "I'm not gonna do it."

"I didn't say you should," he says. But he's studying my face, and I can tell he's picturing me without hair.

After Octavius leaves, I'm lying on the couch reading a novel that isn't about cancer while Mom moves frantically about one of the dress forms standing near me. She's pinning, stepping back to assess it, then moving in again, repeat.

"I have a customer coming any second," she says through the corner of her mouth. Three pins are held between her lips.

"Are you asking me to leave?"

She turns toward me, takes the pins from her mouth. "Why would you think that?"

My shoulders sag. "I never get to see you anymore."

Mom tilts her head. She gives me a sympathetic look.

The doorbell buzzes.

She quickly turns back to the dress form. "Could you get that?"

I sigh, rise to my feet, move to the button on the wall.

"Yes?" I say in a voice that's nearly too cheerful.

"It's Marjorie, for the dress," comes a voice through the speaker.

"Come on up." I hold down the buzzer for three seconds. Then I look to Mom. "Did you want me to leave the room?"

"No, I was just letting you know someone was coming. Actually it would be great if you could get the door. And I'd love to have you stay in the living room."

Seconds later we hear footfalls on the stairs, the landing. Then comes the knock on the door. I step over, open it.

There in the doorway is not just Marjorie—the woman on the intercom—but also a girl, who looks to be about my age. They both smile.

"Hello," I say.

"Hello!" they answer.

They both are dressed fashionably and have beautiful coffee-colored skin. But I'm stricken by the girl, who beneath her blueberry-colored beret is bald. She's who the dress is for.

"El, please invite them in!" Mom says, hurrying

toward the door. I back away as they step in, but I can't look away from the girl as she moves past. Her eyebrows have been wiped away by chemo and drawn back with makeup. She's not trying to be dramatic like Miss Numero Uno. She's just trying to look like a normal, healthy girl who hasn't lost her eyebrows to chemotherapy.

I stand back and watch as Mom plays host, serves them tea, gets the dress from a rack, and presents it to the girl. The girl says it's beautiful, says she loves it, and is escorted by Mom to the bathroom to try it on.

Only when the girl is in the bathroom and Mom is chatting with the mother on the couch do I feel like I can breathe properly. Something about the girl— her age, her demeanor—makes me feel like she's my friend, but a friend who is suddenly less recognizable because of disease. It makes me *want* to be her friend. But it makes me scared to be her friend, because I'm already worried enough about Echo.

After a moment the girl comes out of the bathroom. She looks giddy, she twirls. Her mother applauds, my mother beams. The girl is stunning.

"Look!" she says, unbuttoning the flap where the chemo will be accessed. "It's so cute! And it'll be so easy!" Then she turns to her mom, hand on her heart. "It makes me feel like I'm still *me*."

"I'm so happy you like it," Mom says. She looks really happy and proud of herself. I'm proud of her, too. Then she turns to Marjorie. "I understand how expensive treatment can be, and the last thing I want to do is pile on more financial stress. So, if the price makes life more difficult, I'll accept a lesser amount. You can pay as much as the full price, or as little as my expenses, which for this dress is only about twenty dollars' worth of materials."

The woman's eyes get big, and it's her turn to put her hand to her heart. "For such a beautiful dress? That is *so* generous of you!"

Mom smiles and looks to me. "The sliding scale was actually El's idea." She looks really proud of me.

Now the whole room is smiling at me. The sliding scale seemed like a good idea at the time, but now I'm thinking how with twenty bucks we'll be lucky to pay for one lunch. But whatever.

"Can I wear it home?" the girl asks.

"Of course!" Mom says. She and Marjorie stand and speak to each other quietly. The woman bends over our coffee table to write a check.

The girl comes over to me. She's exactly my height. "You're so lucky to have such a talented mother!"

"Yes," I say.

"Does she make dresses for you?"

"Sometimes." Mom and the woman are at the door, thanking each other. The girl is still standing before me, smiling. "Good luck," I say.

"Thank you!" she says. And hugs me. Hugs *me.*

They exit, the door closes. As their footsteps sound down the stairs, I say a prayer in my head for the girl, even though I don't do that sort of thing.

Mom sighs. "They were nice, weren't they?"

"Yes."

Then she holds up the check the woman gave her, studying it. Now *her* hand goes to her heart.

"What?" I ask.

"Apparently my price doesn't make life more difficult for them."

"That's good."

Mom hands me the check. I feel my eyes get big, to take in the number written on it. It's the price of the dress, plus ten thousand dollars. Which is, like, twenty times what she ordinarily gets for a dress.

On the memo line is written *Thx 4 yr generosity!*

13

MONDAY IN ART class I'm doing a watercolor self-portrait. Miss Numero Uno has assigned us a ton of self-portrait work, which might be because she thinks we need to be more introspective, or possibly because she wants to make things difficult. Doing it in watercolor is the worst.

I'm rendering myself bald, 'cause hair is tricky with watercolor. I look like a character from some science-fiction movie. But I also look like Echo.

Then a shadow falls over my work. I look over my shoulder and see Miss Numero Uno. She has one eyebrow drawn into an arc to indicate interest, but it's just the charcoal stick.

"I am actually interested in your work," she says. "It

is not merely the fact of my eyebrow rendered in the black charcoal stick."

Then she drops a piece of paper on my table and walks away.

I look at the paper. It's a flyer, which reads:

FUND-RAISER FOR ECHO
Cancer has struck a six-year-old girl.
The art world will strike back with a glorious
expression of strength and beauty.
The most avant-garde of New York's visual artists
have donated work, with proceeds benefitting
Echo's medical expenses.
Tar Soup Gallery, SoHo.
Friday, October 28 at 7:00 p.m.

Even though it shows a thoughtfulness, I don't know how to respond to this version of Miss Numero Uno. So I avoid eye contact with her even more than usual, and when the final bell rings I slip out of the classroom.

After dinner I show the flyer to Mom and Dad, though not in that order—I show it to Dad and he shares it with Mom. Then later in the evening, after Echo has gone to bed and I'm working on homework in the kitchen, they call me into the living room.

They're sitting on the couch with one space between them. I sit in the armchair and start twirling my hair.

Mom begins. "This is a very nice gesture from Miss Numero Uno." She holds the flyer up, sets it down. "Please tell her that I would like to contribute a dress to the fund-raiser."

I smile. "Okay."

"*And*," Dad says, "please tell her that I will do my best to come up with a painting in time to contribute."

Immediately I wonder where the heck this is gonna happen. The apartment is already crowded enough, and Dad was known for his large work. But I stay positive. "Cool," I say.

In the week that follows, Dad is absent from the apartment most of the time, but I don't think much of it. Mom is busy making dresses with chemo port access for little girls and grown women and having me run packages to the post office to mail out. She works on her dress for the gallery show after I've gone to bed. Dad gets home from teaching art to preschoolers and kindergarteners and then disappears after dinner.

On Thursday evening, Mom is finishing the dress she's contributing to the fund-raiser. It's short and made of waterproof shipping envelopes. They're white with bits of black and red and blue printed on them. There are also address labels here and there with actual addresses written on them. The pieces are joined with stitching where she's doubled over the rip-proof paper for extra strength. I had my doubts as to how it would turn out, but it looks really, really cool.

Then I remember Dad was going to contribute a piece, and ask him about it.

"I'll show you after dinner."

The four of us dine on spinach enchiladas with pomegranate seeds as a side, made and brought to us by a woman Mom used to do yoga with. After I do the dishes, which has suddenly become my chore, the four of us put on our shoes and head out the door.

Dad leads us downstairs and outside our apartment building, then into the basement. The landlord lives in an apartment that's six steps down from the street. The other half of the basement is taken up by the laundry room.

We enter to warm air and the smell of fabric softener, like fake flowers. Mom and Echo and I all gasp, as immediately we are confronted with a giant painting, on a board about seven feet wide and four feet high, of a woman in a gown reclined on a couch. Except it's not really a painting, or at least there isn't any paint on it.

The entire surface is covered with scraps of newspaper glued into place, and the scraps with wider expanses of black ink have been arranged to make a line drawing. The red outline of the couch is made from the red ink of newspaper advertisements. The couch and the reclining woman look like they're trying to soak up the entire area of the board.

Altogether it looks amazing. Mom leans into Dad and puts her arm around him. "Brings back memories," she says.

At this moment, I'm so proud of Mom and Dad, for the dress and this giant painting made of newspaper scraps. Maybe they don't make as much money as some other parents, but they can do *this*.

"I just have to cover it with clear acrylic," Dad says, "and then it'll be ready to go."

He puts a key in the door of a storage closet that has decals with our unit number, 3A. He opens the door and reveals a small closet filled with art materials—cans of gesso and paint, and bottles of paint, and rolls of canvas, and tubes of glue. Everything looks old.

"Have you had this stuff all along?" I ask.

Dad turns to me and smiles. "Yep. And I've been away from it for too long."

I look at Dad and Mom and I imagine them as a younger couple, living in a closet in the Village and starving together this way. I can see why it seems romantic to them to remember it. Because it seems romantic to me.

Late at night after finishing my homework, I climb quietly into the upper bunk so as not to wake Echo. But then her voice sounds in the darkness.

"El?"

"Yeah?"

"Am I still me?"

I wait for her to expand on her question, but she doesn't. "Of course you are."

"I look different and I feel different and I never get to do the things I used to do."

I lean over the edge and look at her. She's scowling sadly at my mattress above her. "You're still my little sister," I say. "You still make me laugh."

I hope that she'll smile at what I've said, but she doesn't. So I ask, "Are you excited about the fund-raiser party tomorrow night?"

Her brow furrows. "Is everyone mad at me for my cancer being so expensive?"

I'm shocked. *"No."* I climb down the ladder and kneel at her bedside. "You beating cancer is the most important thing for all of us."

She's still staring at the bunk above, looking

unhappy. I put my hand on the top of her smooth head.

"What happens if I don't beat cancer?"

This hits me like a truck. But it's my turn to be the strong one, so my face, my expression, remains unchanged.

"Not gonna happen. You're kicking cancer's butt because you do everything the doctors ask you to do. You take all the medicines and you eat healthy foods, and you've got a great attitude. When cancer sees you laughing and being silly, it wants to run and hide."

This makes her smile. "Good. 'Cause I don't wanna die."

It's hard for me to keep smiling when she says this, but I will myself to. Somewhere in my heart I've known that she understands the stakes, the size of the beast she's fighting. Every now and then she proves it to me.

"Someday, far in the future," I say. "But not tonight."

"First I wanna be a cartoonist, and have a French bulldog, and be a mom, and I wanna be an aunt when you have kids. And then I wanna be a granny!" She starts laughing.

I smile. "That laugh! Cancer has just left the building."

"Lock the door!" More laughter.

I kiss her on the forehead, then climb back up to my bunk. Lying on my back I think of how much braver she has become, and how much stronger. I think about how I'll explain this to her, that she's still Echo, only now she's a warrior princess. But when I look back down to her face, her eyes are closed and she's breathing evenly.

✿ ✿ ✿

The next day after school I'm up in the Garment District, running errands for Mom. The Garment District is an area of Manhattan where all the stores sell things needed by clothing designers. There'll be a store with nothing but feather boas next to a store that sells only gold lamé. I first visit a store that sells buttons and then a store that sells zippers, both for Mom's chemo dress line. She's staying busy with it, which means I'm not as worried about us being homeless, but which also means the home we *have*, and particularly the living room, is filled with three or four dress forms at a time, standing like headless guests at a dull party.

Heading home, the things I picked up for Mom are practically weightless, but my book bag filled with school texts is dragging me down. I'm hoping I'll have a chance to rest before Miss Numero Uno's gallery fund-raiser tonight.

When I get off the train at the Washington Square station, I hear the piano. It's been ages since I've been in this station—we were here every day when Echo was in the hospital. With Echo home we haven't ventured outside the neighborhood much, so it's been a while since I've seen the piano guy.

I have to walk right past him to get to the stairs. He's wearing an unbuttoned, forest green cardigan over a comic book T-shirt. His dirty-blond hair is pulled back in a short ponytail. Though my first thought was to get by him quickly before he notices me, I find myself taking slow steps.

"Hey!" he shouts, and bangs on the keys. "Long time, no see!"

I've halted, standing ten feet from him. "Long time, no hear."

He scoots to the left side of his bench. "You owe me a duet."

Sheepishly I smile. I could use a rest. There wasn't a free seat on the subway, and I've been walking all over the Garment District. So I sit on the bench, to his right.

He plays four quick notes. "As I recall, you said you had trouble with your left hand."

"Yep."

"Well," he says, and pats me on the back, "I'm happy

to lend you one of mine. I'll play left and you play right. Sound good?"

"It might," I say. "We can try."

"The last time I saw you I played 'Everything Happens to Me' at your request."

"You've got a good memory."

He smiles. "Well, it's not every day a schoolgirl requests a mighty standard like that. Shall we play it like Thelonious Monk?"

I smile. "You play it like Monk and I'll play it like a seventh grader whose instruction has been spotty."

He nudges me. "Just peck it out on your right hand, and my left hand will be here for harmony."

I sigh. Not an unhappy sigh, or an exhausted sigh. More like the sigh of someone about to be revealed as sucking at something.

My right hand goes to the keyboard. I hit one note, the first. Piano Guy follows with his left hand, but I've kept my next space empty.

"Try that again," he says. "But this time don't stop. And remember it doesn't have to be perfect. Just keep playing through it, whatever happens."

"Keep playing through it," I repeat. It sounds like a cancer mantra. "Whatever happens."

I stretch my hand. I hit the first note, and follow it with the next.

Piano Guy is right beside me. I'm surprised at the sensation of having him there, steady and in time. It's like I'm having a dream that I can play the piano really well.

We play on. I've never gotten this far into the song before, and didn't know I even knew it well enough.

We're two parts of one whole. I laugh, because I *get* it. I get why people are in bands, why they jam. But I also get that two brains on one instrument is something else. Like we're conjoined twins.

As we keep playing it, I feel like my heart is swelling. Like it's gonna burst. Even when I screw up, he picks me up, and it sounds amazing.

Finally we near the end. It's like watching myself walking on a high wire, and I've almost made it to the finish. I just want to run the last few steps, but he keeps me from changing pace, from charging ahead.

Then we're there. He leans against me, nudging me toward the end of the keyboard, and I can hear in my head how Monk exits this song. I hit the key at the far right, the highest C, once, then three times in rapid succession. It sounds perfectly out of tune.

When I look up from the keyboard I feel like I'm soaring as high as that last note. There are five or six people gathered to watch, which almost never happens—actually stopping to watch and listen at rush hour—and they begin clapping. Some of them feed the jar, then they move on to catch their trains or go home to their cats and dinners. I turn to Piano Guy, and he looks into my eyes with a wild happiness, which I know I'm mirroring back at him.

"That was too much fun!" he says. "You were great!"

"Thank you! So were you!"

Being so exhilarated is exhausting. And I feel a little weird being so happy.

"I have to get home," I say, rising from the bench.

"Wait." He reaches beneath the bench for a small cloth sack and puts it over the top of his tip jar. Then he turns the jar over to empty it into the sack. He pulls the cord at the top to tighten it and hands it to me. "For Echo's medical expenses."

My mind does a quick review of my family's history with Piano Guy. "How did you know about Echo?"

He reaches to the right and strikes the highest C. "I live in the neighborhood. Even in a city as big as New York, when you sit in the same place long enough, the faces start looking familiar. I remember you guys all getting on the subway together, and now it's just you and your pops. But I've seen Echo's face on the jars at the bodega. At all the other businesses. How can I not admire the strength of a kid like that? And a kid like *you*, being there for her every day."

I can't believe he included me in that. "That means a lot coming from a guy who hauls his piano everywhere."

He drops a finger on the lowest D key. "This thing is nothing."

"I don't know what to say." My heart swells like it did when we were playing together. "*Thank* you."

He smiles. "Thank *you*. For hearing the music. For stopping to listen. You're my audience, so I get to make a living playing the piano. And how cool is that?" He plays a ditty with his left hand and tips an imaginary hat at me with his right.

"What's your name?" I ask.

"A-Train Eddie." He extends his hand to me.

"El," I say, giving him mine. He has long fingers, and my hand disappears in his.

"Ah, like the old train! That can be your jazz name. *Third Avenue El.*"

I have no idea what he's talking about. And we live between Sixth and Seventh, but I smile. "Thanks for everything," I say, though it sounds terribly inadequate. "I hope to hear you soon!"

"Keep practicing, Third Avenue El. Let's play again, okay?"

"Okay," I say. And I know I absolutely mean it.

Then A-Train Eddie puts his hands to the keyboard,

nods to me, and walks me out with "Sunny Side of the Street."

It's the absolute perfect song for right now. It's exactly what I need.

I hear it as I climb the steps out of the subway station. I hear it as I enter the world above.

I hear it over the taxi horns and the town cars streaming north on Sixth Avenue.

I hear it all the long walk home.

14

IT'S FINALLY TIME for the gallery fund-raiser, and Echo can't even go. She can't go because she has a fever of 101.6.

We found this out as we were getting ready. Mom kissed Echo on her forehead, then drew back with a look of concern, putting her hand to Echo's brow. The thermometer gave the final verdict. So now Echo gets to wear her wonderful pink party dress—which Mom made for the occasion—in the emergency room.

It's the stinking protocol.

There's gonna be a few hundred people packed into the gallery. Everything is paid for, everyone is on their way. So Dad and I will be the ambassadors of gloom. Mom and Echo will be the ones who have to endure missing out.

Mom and Dad asked me to say something to the people who come to the fund-raiser. They think it'll be good for me. And now I'm looking at my speech and modifying it, editing, as Dad and I ride the cab from the emergency room to the party in SoHo. I strike the line *Doesn't Echo look beautiful in her pink party dress?*

When we get to the gallery, we find the ornate cast-iron facade of the building is strung with yellow lights. It looks festive. It would make Echo very happy to see it, which makes me miserable to think.

"Remember to smile," Dad says as we get out of the cab. "We want everyone to know how grateful we are."

The party is already well under way. There's a big blown-up photograph of Echo on one of the walls, along with massive reproductions of some of her drawings printed on canvas, which Mom supplied to Miss Numero Uno. They look pretty cool on such a large scale.

And there are paintings of all sizes by a couple of dozen different artists. There are all sorts of styles and subjects represented, on canvas and panel, in acrylic and oil, figurative and abstract. Then I spot Dad's piece. I grab him by the arm and pull him to it.

Hanging on the wall, with good light, instead of in the dim basement with the smell of fabric softener from the laundry, it looks even more impressive.

I soak it in, then turn to him and smile. I'm so, so proud of him. He looks proud of himself.

Then I move in to look at the tag on the wall next to it. The price he chose for it—a thousand dollars—has been crossed out and replaced with two thousand dollars. There's a red dot next to it.

"What does the red dot mean?" I ask.

Dad looks from me to the tag. He squints and moves in closer. "That means somebody bought it. And it looks like they raised the price."

"That's great!"

He nods. "That *is* pretty great." Then he turns to me. "I've been thinking. I don't know if I want to get a master's and teach college kids. I don't even believe you can be taught at that age."

I furrow my brow. "Then what will you do?"

He turns toward his painting, opens his arms to it. *"This."* He smiles at me. "I did it before, I can do it again." Then he leans to me and whispers, *"And teaching toddlers how to hold a paintbrush."*

I smile, because this makes me happy. It also terrifies me, but mostly it makes me happy.

I pull his arm and begin looking for red dots on the price labels of other paintings. They're everywhere. More paintings have a red dot than not. The prices are often even higher than Dad's painting. It makes my head spin to think of how much money it adds up to.

We come to a naked mannequin standing beside the wall. The mannequin is supposed to be wearing Mom's dress, but the red dot on the tag on the wall beside it shows it has been purchased. Five thousand dollars for a dress! That's more than we spend on clothes in our family in a year. But I'm so proud of Mom. It really was beautiful, and *so* worth the price. One of a kind, handmade in Manhattan by my amazingly talented mom. I hope she took some pictures of it.

The house music is playing the Echo's Fight Song sampler originally put together by Octavius, which Dad shared with Miss Numero Uno at my suggestion. The sound fills the huge space up to its soaring ceilings.

We're spotted by Gwen, the gallery owner. She's wearing ridiculously high heels and a string of enormous pearls over a red Team Echo T-shirt and black leather skirt. She gives me a hug and one of those fake cheek kisses, then does the same to Dad. I stay by his side as we walk through the crowd, greeting people, thanking people.

The Team Echo T-shirts are everywhere, mixed with expensive high-fashion clothing. They're worn by people we know and people who look familiar, and people who I'm sure I've never laid eyes on. Octavius has evidently been conspiring without telling me. But I can live with this kind of conspiring.

The people we speak with ask where Echo is, and we give them the bad news. Lots of shiny, happy faces turn to disappointment. But the collective spirit remains high.

Then the music fades, and there's the sound of a microphone being tapped. A woman's voice, which seems familiar, fills the gallery.

"Good evening."

On a small stage stands a woman wearing Wayfarer sunglasses, heels, and—Mom's dress! She certainly has the figure for it, and she looks terrific.

"There once was a young couple who lived in a cramped and poorly lit space in the Village. The young man was a painter, the young woman a dressmaker. Though they had little money, they created works of art that filled their otherwise bleak existences with meaning."

It hits me. The woman wearing Mom's dress is Miss Numero Uno. But she's either dyed her hair blue or she's wearing a wig.

"As they lived and created, they met others like themselves. People whose sustenance was the art they made."

She strikes a dramatic pose, as if she's reacting to a canvas she's just painted. Or like she's standing back and admiring a dress form decked out in a new design. It's *definitely* Miss Numero Uno.

"Whenever there was a fund-raiser, they could be counted on. Donating a painting to help pay for stolen art supplies. Donating a dress to help someone fight eviction from their apartment. They did it often and without hesitation."

I look to Dad. I didn't know this about my parents.

"Grace makes dresses that are perhaps a bit sunny for my tastes, yet I have surrendered three weeks' pay to support her daughter. And I look spectacular in it, do I not?"

The crowd howls and applauds. I hear myself whistle, I see my hands clapping furiously as she spins on the stage, modeling it.

"Tate still hasn't learned to draw, but he renders his subjects in a style that takes one's breath away, does he not?"

The crowd erupts as she extends an arm to indicate Dad's painting. Dad laughs and does a little bow.

"I teach the older daughter, El." She looks at me directly, curiously. "Or does she teach me? She produces work to be encouraged."

The crowd cheers as she points to a painting I hadn't noticed before. It's my painting of Echo getting chemo! Or rather the drawing I made, blown up into a huge silkscreen.

"And behold the work of Echo! She is expression personified."

The crowd cheers as Miss Numero Uno points to a large silkscreen reproduction of Echo's *Miss you hair* drawing.

"This girl, and this family, is worth fighting for. Let us help carry their burden!"

Then she pulls off her blue wig and flings it to the audience. Her head is *bare*.

"This family is worth our sacrifice!"

The crowd goes wild. She steps off the stage like a runway model and heads to the table covered in glasses filled with wine.

I can't believe what I've just witnessed. I can't believe *any* of this.

Gwen, the gallery owner, takes the stage and leans to the microphone.

"Now please welcome Echo's older sister, El."

A loud round of applause. What did I do to deserve a round of applause?

I'm afraid to step up to the mic and earn it. But Dad pats me on the back.

I adjust the microphone, tilting it down. I'm suddenly aware of my party dress, which feels frivolous, so I try to hide as much of myself as possible behind the podium. But all eyes are directed at me.

The applause quiets.

"Hello."

My voice sounds strange over the speakers. A few jolly people say hello back.

"As some of you already know, Echo isn't able to make it tonight."

I give the crowd a second to react. Sympathetic groans and sighs.

"That completely sucks. So she's wearing a pink party dress and a cute headband with a bow, but she's wearing it at the emergency room, because her temperature is 101.6."

An arm waves from the back of the crowd. It's Octavius. I smile a half smile and raise my hand to give him a shy wave.

"Hi, Octavius. Thanks for bringing the T-shirts."

Saying this almost breaks me up. People applaud.

"So, Echo was excited to see you all and to thank you for everything you've done for her and our family, but instead you get to hear Echo's sister."

I look to the sheet in my hand, my prepared speech that's been held in my clenched fist the whole time we've been here. I uncrumple it as best I can and begin reading into the microphone.

"The day Echo went into the hospital was the first day of school. Before my dad and I went to go visit her at the hospital we had Chinese takeout at home. I wanted to see my fortune cookie because I hoped it would tell me that everything was going to be okay with Echo. But when I opened it up, the little strip of paper was completely blank."

I unscrew the cap of the little water bottle I'm holding and take a sip.

"At the time I felt annoyed, and cheated. So I asked for my dad's fortune cookie, but his wasn't a fortune. It was a reminder that the restaurant did catering."

A few people laugh.

"Looking back at it, I think the fortune in my cookie was blank because there's no way you could fit everything that was about to happen on one tiny slip of paper. Or it was blank because even if it did tell me, there was no way I would believe it, or understand it."

I take another sip of water and clear my throat.

"El!" It's Maisy, waving as she pushes forward in the crowd, her mother behind her.

"Hi, Maisy!" I wave back and blow her a kiss. I watch her for a moment, feeling how great it is to have her back in my heart. My eyes return to the page. "I didn't know how strong Echo is. I didn't know how funny she is, or how much I love her. Or how much I would ache for her when she was in the hospital. How much she would teach me. She's taught me *so* many things. Especially with how she hasn't let cancer keep her from being a kid. She tries to have fun as much as she can, always."

I take another sip of water.

"I didn't know how creative my mom is. Or how fierce her love is for Echo and me. And how my dad puts us before everything."

My brow furrows to fight back tears.

"But I was most surprised by all of you. I didn't know how *great* humanity could be. Echo has met everything with such bravery, and you told us it was because she had such a strong family supporting her. But we were only as strong as we've been because we've had all of *you* carrying us."

I wipe my eyes with the back of my hand.

"Your prayers, your vibes, your healing thoughts, your juju, your love. Your fund-raisers. Your gifts. You wouldn't let us buy our own ice cream."

My voice cracks. I wait for my composure to return before speaking again.

"You cooked us dinners and brought them to our apartment. Including the most amazing daal I've ever tasted. I can't stop thinking about that daal."

I crack up a bit. I really can't stop thinking about the daal.

"You told us that we were good people and that we were always valued members of the community. You told us it was karma that everything we gave would come back to us. You said such nice things about our family, it made me wonder whether what you said was true."

It's true, comes a small chorus from the crowd. I can't see the people in front of me, because I can't look at them.

"When Echo got her diagnosis, my dad came up with a slogan to remind us to take care of each other. *All for one, all four one.* I thought it was cheesy and ridiculous at first, but then I began seeing how important it was for all four of us in our family to eat right, and sleep well, and exercise, and laugh, and pick each other up when one of us was down."

I take a sip of water.

"But none of us had any idea how much of the heavy lifting all of you would do for us. So, thank you. Thank you for loving us. Thank you for lifting our spirits. Thank you for everything."

I raise my eyes and make an effort to see the faces through my tears.

"Right now I feel so lucky to be a member of this species, and this community." I sweep my arm to indicate the beautiful tear-blurred people before me. "And I'm so incredibly proud to be Echo's sister."

I lift my water bottle high. "To humanity."

"To humanity!" the crowd calls back with glasses raised. It's really something.

"To Echo!" someone shouts.

"To Echo!" comes the louder echo. It's really something else.

Then, smiling, I lean in to the microphone.

"It may be twenty years or so away, but I'm sure Echo won't mind my saying that every last one of you is invited to her wedding."

Everyone laughs. Then everyone applauds as I turn from the podium and see my dad, who's been standing there all along. His face shiny, he grins at me. He steps up to the podium and bends down to the microphone.

"I echo El's sentiments."

Everyone laughs again, and then Dad points to the woman at the music and gives her a thumbs-up. "Lust for Life" rises on the speakers, and I take Dad's hand in mine and lead him to the floor, where we dance together just like we will at my wedding, and just like he'll dance with Echo at hers.

Late at night I'm in bed staring at the stars on the ceiling above me. From outside the bedroom I hear the door to our apartment open, and Dad quietly greeting Mom and Echo as they return from the emergency room. Standard procedure is to pump her port full of antibiotics and wait for her fever to come down, then send her home at whatever hour.

I hear the bathroom sink and the electric toothbrush, then the light from the hall spills into the room as Echo enters. She falls into bed with a groan.

I lean over the edge and look down to her.

"Good night, Echo."

Her eyes are open, but she doesn't say anything. It's perfectly okay for her to be too tired and grumpy to say good night back to me.

I roll back on my bed. It isn't fair that I'm the one feeling the glow from the love, from the fun of the party. It should be Echo who gets to feel it.

I glare at the stars on the ceiling and think of how heartless the universe is. It's filled with loving people, but the universe has no heart and no sense of fairness. I think this until I feel it in my core. Then I sit up and climb down the ladder to the floor. I gaze at Echo's sleeping form, watching for the rise and fall of her chest by the light of the alarm clock.

Then I slip out the door.

First I enter the living room. I open the closet near the front door, and in the dim light see the keyboard standing on its end behind a box of books. I push the books aside, drag the keyboard out, stand it on its unfolded legs in front of a bookcase, and plug it in. I turn the volume dial down, then hit the highest C note—once, then three times in rapid succession. It sounds almost as magical as when I played with A-Train Eddie.

It's never going back in the closet.

I turn the power switch off and walk into the bathroom. I stare at myself in the mirror. I look at my long dark hair. I run my fingers through it.

Then I open the drawer.

I take the scissors, hang my head down over the sink, and gather my hair. I cut as close to my scalp as I can. It's more difficult than I imagined.

When I'm done, I raise my head and look in the mirror. My hair is short and messy, uneven, like someone had a sneezing fit while trimming it. I look like my doll did when I was five and cut her hair.

It's not what you would call stylish. It's not even punk rock.

I walk into the kitchen and get a ziplock freezer bag to put the hair into. Let it become a wig for a kid doing chemo who wants her hair. She can have mine.

I leave it on the kitchen counter and return to the bathroom, take the hair trimmer from the drawer, and plug it in. I turn it on and begin buzzing what's left, back and forth, feeling with my free hand. I gather the fallen hair from the sink and throw it into the toilet, then flush it.

Finally I look in the mirror again.

I look strange, but maybe I see myself as beautiful, if I can be allowed to think that. I look like a character from some science fiction movie. I also look like Echo.

It's like I'm her big sidekick. But I could be worse things than that.

I stare at myself for a while. Then I turn off the light and climb into bed.

In the darkness, I smile at how I've made the universe a little bit more just, a little more fair. I tilted the scales by the smallest measure.

The stars painted on my ceiling look down on me admiringly.

15

IN SPITE OF how great Friday was—with A-Train
Eddie and the gallery fund-raiser—Monday morning,
walking the halls at school, I feel even more like a mis-
fit. It's been an unhappy place for me since the end of
day one, but today it feels even more like everyone is
looking at me. Or that they're trying hard *not* to look
at me. They stop talking when I walk by. They either
stare at me or they look away when I come into view.

My newly bald head is beneath a knitted wool cap.
I'm not looking forward to the reveal.

Part of me wishes I hadn't shaved it. Echo *laughed.*
It's not like she fell all over herself thanking me. But
why would she? It's like I was punishing myself for not
having cancer.

Just before I get to Mr. D's classroom, I've had

enough. A random boy stares at me like I'm some kind of freak-show attraction.

"What?" I stare him down as I pass. He turns away to his open locker.

I trudge into Mr. D's class and fall into my front-row seat. Mr. D smiles at me from where he sits on the edge of his desk, and one corner of my mouth twitches in response.

It seems strangely quiet as everyone takes their seats. Maybe they're all nervous about getting their papers back. I can't even remember what the assignment was.

When the bell rings, Mr. D drops from the desk to his feet and approaches the front of the class. He stops a couple steps from my desk.

"Good morning, class." He's looking handsome in a navy sweater and khakis. "I hope everyone had a good weekend."

He begins pacing back and forth. "The assignment was simple. Write something where the narrative voice, or protagonist, experiences surprise. As a class, you did wonderful work. But one . . ."

Mr. D turns from the class and quickly fetches some papers from a folder on his desk. He holds the stapled assignment in his outstretched hand. I follow his eyes to Sydney, the girl who sits to my left. She

sits slunk down in her chair—the girl who has com-
plained anytime Mr. D liked my work, the girl who
saw me getting gelato with Echo and then apparently
told the whole school that my sister has cancer, so
that instead of being ignored now I am treated like a
freak show.

Sydney.

I look away from her, back to Mr. D. He still holds
the paper in front of himself, his eyebrows slightly
raised.

Just as I notice the sound of the fluorescent lights
humming overhead, she sits up in her chair, then
stands. Her body language communicates dread as
she walks slowly to where Mr. D waits. He hands the
paper to her, pats her on the shoulder, and goes to sit
in his chair behind his desk.

I look at her like I'm seeing her for the first time.
It's almost like I could be looking at myself—same
uniform skirt and shirt, similar brown hair hanging
in her face, obscuring it, which is exactly how I feel.

Then I remember I don't have any hair. I reach up
and touch my knitted cap.

"The day I first saw you," she begins, reading from
her paper, "I imagined you were very much like myself."

Her hands are trembling, rattling the pages. To my
surprise I'm not enjoying her discomfort.

"Your clothes were just like mine, ha-ha."

It's a joke, but she says it flatly. Some of the kids behind me laugh.

"But then I realized you wore the uniform better than I did. *Much* better. And I *hated* you for it."

The class falls silent.

"I listened to you speak, in response to our teacher, and I thought you sounded very much like me. You said things I wished I had said. Finally I realized you were much smarter than me, and I *hated* you for it."

I hear someone's shoes squeaking in the hallway outside, running past.

"I put myself close to you. I hoped that you would notice me and want to be my friend. But you never looked up. You never noticed me or anyone else in class. You seemed to be perfectly independent, above the pettiness of seventh grade. And I *hated* you for it."

If I hadn't been completely unable to connect with my schoolmates, I might be able to guess who she was talking about.

"You were prettier than me, and smarter than me, and unlike myself, you didn't need anyone. I hated you for *all* of these things."

She brushes her hair behind her left ear, so one whole side of her face is now visible. Her cheek is streaked with tears.

"Then one day I saw you with your sister. She was like a younger version of your perfect self. But she was sick. *Very* sick."

She looks to me over her paper, her eyes filled with pain.

My jaw drops. *She's talking about me.*

"There, in a gelato shop, with your bald-headed sister, instead of seeing you as a girl who was so perfect she needed nobody and nothing, I saw someone who was vulnerable. And I hated *myself* for it."

Her face is contorted with anguish.

"I saw that you, the girl I admired and then envied and hated, were troubled beyond anything I'd ever experienced, and I hated *myself* for it."

I'm suddenly very hot, and I pull off the knitted cap. Sydney's hand goes to her heart.

"I hated myself for everything I had thought about you. I hated myself for completely misreading you. I hated myself for my insecurity. For my mean-spirited, petty jealousy."

She looks from the paper to my face. It's like the rest of the class is no longer in the room. Like she's reading it for me only.

"Stalking your family on Facebook, I learned about your sister's cancer. *Six years old.* I learned about all the money fears. I learned how much health insurance sucks. How you were worried you'd have to leave this school, and Manhattan, and that there wouldn't be enough money for the surgeries, the hospital stays, and all the medicine. I learned how hard this was for all of you as a family."

I feel cool air on my bare head, and I realize I've unveiled it without much ado.

"I saw you in the gelato shop. I saw a stranger pay for your gelato. I saw it with my own eyes, you and your little sister, and I saw the humble graciousness with which you accepted his gift. I saw jars with her name and sweet face at bodegas in the neighborhood, and restaurants, put out by the business owners who loved you."

She pushes the other half of her hair behind her right ear and looks at me with directness.

"I have a little sister, too. Her name is Adelaide."

She smiles, but her head shakes with crying. I become conscious of myself, and I decide that I must just look stunned.

Sydney's eyes go back to the paper.

"Sometimes even the strongest people are given too much to carry. I wanted to help, but I'm just a seventh-grade girl who apparently sucks at everything. But I have a few friends. And they have other friends. We all have parents. And cousins in other states."

A big tear falls from her cheek and smacks the paper in her hands.

"Thirty-seven states. Plus the District of Columbia. And five foreign countries."

She blots her face with her forearm.

"I was surprised how raising a bunch of money still left me feeling like I didn't do enough. I couldn't help take away your family's *biggest* worry."

She fidgets with the top button of her shirt.

"But I was surprised at how beautiful humanity can be."

Me too. I mouth the words to her.

"I was surprised to find that you weren't who I thought you were. I was surprised that I admired you even more than I had previously. And that I wanted to be your friend more than ever."

Me too.

"But I haven't figured out how to tell you."

Her arms fall to her sides. The paper falls to the floor. She laughs, because she couldn't figure out how to tell me, but she just told me in front of the entire class. Thanks to Mr. D making her read her assignment aloud.

I stand. I approach Sydney and put my arms around her, this girl who I completely misread. I feel her arms go around me, and we hold the pose for a moment before someone in the rows of desks begins clapping. The two hands are joined by more pairs until the entire class is clapping. I can't pull away from Sydney because I don't want everyone to see what's become of my face—I'm so happy I must certainly look like I'm miserable—and because hugging her feels so good.

Finally I draw back and wipe my eyes. The clapping subsides.

"I dearly wish to be your friend, Sydney. And I'm *so* grateful to have you on Team Echo."

She smiles, and looks to Mr. D. He stands.

"Well, since you've brought up Team Echo," begins Mr. D, "I hope you have room in the bleachers for a few more."

Sydney unbuttons her blue uniform shirt from the top down, revealing a red Team Echo T-shirt beneath.

Octavius!

I smile. I hear a commotion and look around the room. Half the kids in my class, boys and girls alike, are taking off their uniform shirts to reveal Team Echo shirts. The ones who aren't are smiling.

I feel like I'm seeing everyone's faces for the first time. All these smiling girls and guys.

I can't wait to meet these kids.

I turn to Mr. D. "Can we please have a round of

applause for Sydney's incredibly well-done assign-ment?"

"Hear, hear!" says Mr. D, who has stripped off his navy sweater to reveal the red tee. "A round of applause for Sydney's paper!"

Everyone in class applauds with an enthusiasm for academic work not often seen from seventh graders.

Sydney looks like she's just won the lottery. In fact she's just won the lottery for Echo. I give her another hug, then take a step back and hold out my hand.

"Hello, Sydney. My name is El, but my *real* name is Laughter. I'm so happy to meet you."

Sydney laughs, bright-eyed, as her warm hand shakes mine. Then she uses the fingertips of both hands to wipe away her tears "I'm so happy to meet Laughter, El."

We come together for another hug.

"Wow," says Mr. D, and drops into his chair. "That was an above-average moment for seventh-grade English."

A couple of hours later I'm sitting in the cafeteria, eat-ing lunch with Sydney. My new friend. She's sharing her broiled asparagus spears with me.

"Oh," she says, and reaches for her backpack on the floor. She unzips it, reaches inside for a pen and paper.

She writes a phone number, then a dollar sign and a five-digit number. "This is my mom's phone number, and this is the amount of money we raised. My mom says we should wire it to your parents' account, so please ask them to call her."

My mouth is hanging open. "I can't even believe this. This is so generous of you."

She shakes her head. "This came from a whole lot of people. And please don't ever mention it again. I'd prefer if you didn't even think of it. You and me are even Steven."

I look at her eyes, then through the tall cafeteria windows and back to her. "*Thank* you."

She smiles and reaches her hand to mine. "That'll do."

Octavius glides by with a tray of food. He smiles sidelong at me as he passes, and I smile back. He's letting me have this lunch with just Sydney, because he's wise and good and kind.

I sigh, then fold the paper twice and tuck it deep into my shirt pocket. Then I reach for my last spear of gift asparagus and take a bite. I look across at Sydney, who looks across at me. I don't say anything about the money, though it's foremost in my thoughts. Then I think how I'm never going to be the same, how I'll never be the same person again after all of this, and I think about the kind of person I want to be. The kind of person who one day will do this, or something like this, for someone else.

"So," Sydney says, leaning over her lunch box toward me. "Tell me about Octavius." She smiles.

"What?" I feel myself blush. "There's nothing to tell. He's just a friend." I look across the cafeteria to where he sits with a group of boys, all wearing red Team Echo shirts. "A really *good* friend." I reach my hand to hers. "Like *you.*"

16

AT THE END of November all the pieces fall into place for Echo to have surgery to remove the tumor. It's shrunk considerably from the weeks of chemotherapy. Her blood numbers are good. The doctor who will make the obturator to replace her teeth and the part of the roof of her mouth that will be cut out has been granted privileges for Midtown Children's Hospital. The oncologist has given her blessing for it to happen. Mom and Dad have paid enough money to make it work. I hear Mom tell Dad all this after Mom gets a call at three p.m. telling her to not give any food or drink to Echo after midnight. Check-in at the hospital is at five thirty in the morning.

Mom packs for a three-night stay—books for Echo and work for herself, and everything she wished she thought of on the first stay in the hospital, when Echo was first diagnosed.

Dad makes my lunch before we have dinner, even though I've been making it myself for weeks. I think he wants to do better than he did last time around. It's sweet to watch. He also sets the second Harry Potter book aside, as he and Echo have finished the first. Then he takes to Facebook and asks everyone to send their well-wishes.

Echo takes a bath and brushes her teeth—some of them for the last time—then is off to an early bed.

I'm too nervous to go right to sleep when I finally go to bed. I stare at the stars on the ceiling. Then I close my eyes, count to ten, and open them. I concentrate on the first fake star I see, the first I lay eyes on.

Star light, star bright,
First star I see tonight,
I wish I may, I wish I might,
Have this wish I wish tonight.

I must be superstitious, because I don't even tell *myself* what I wished for.

The alarm goes off at four forty-five, and everything is ready to go. Dad set the coffeemaker to brew at 4:40, so the coffee is ready to be poured into a thermos for Mom. The bags are ready by the door. Echo slips from her jammies into a cozy winter suit, and Mom dresses warmly for the last day of November.

The taxi has been arranged for 5:10, and he buzzes the door right on time. Dad and I rush down the stairs with Echo and Mom, and when we step out into the dark, cold morning, we are met by a wondrous sight.

The landing and the front steps are lined by candles in tall jars, glowing in the dark of winter's predawn. Dozens of them stand shoulder to shoulder—many with paper notes attached—down to the sidewalk below. This conspiracy of love must be a response to Dad's asking for well-wishing on Facebook.

"It looks like you are very popular," the cabbie says. He opens the door for Echo, but she takes a long look up and down the steps, grinning at the candles, before getting in the taxi. Mom wipes away a tear, then kisses Dad and me.

"Good luck!" Dad says. "I'll be there after I get El to school!"

"Good luck!" I say. "I love you, Echo!"

Then the taxi rolls away down the block.

Dad lets me bring my phone to school, just this once. He promises to text me with any news about Echo's surgery. But it feels like it just makes time pass more slowly.

I have a terrible difficulty concentrating during Mr. D's class, secretly checking my phone every time his back is turned. Sydney seems almost as interested in hearing news as I am. She keeps on looking over at me with a questioning look, and I keep on looking back at her and shrugging.

The wait drags on in math and history. During Mr. Grimm's class I finally can't take it anymore, so I ask to use the bathroom so I can text a series of question marks to Dad. As I sit on the toilet not peeing, Dad's response comes.

Still in surgery. No news yet.

At lunch I sit with Octavius and Sydney, my phone faceup on the table. We make empty small talk between bites of food and glances at my phone. I'm reaching for another carrot stick when finally it buzzes, lighting up the screen. I grab it and spin on the bench seat, turning away from my friends.

I hold it close to my face, keeping it private in my cupped hands.

It melts my eyes. The text message from Dad gives me everything I asked of the first star I saw on the ceiling above my bed last night.

> Surgery went beautifully. They think they got all the
> cancer. Only four teeth removed. Echo is doing fine!

I spin back to Sydney and Octavius. I can't communicate the words. Instead I set the phone down between them so they can see the news. Within seconds we're hugging and blabbering, making happy noises. Then it becomes clear the whole school knew Echo's surgery was today—since pretty much everyone here is Team Echo now—because the whole cafeteria stands and applauds, taking their cue from the three of us that it went well. Practically everyone leaves their seats to take turns hugging me.

Thank you, I say to my classmates. *Thank you.*

Across the cafeteria, Miss Numero Uno appears in the doorway. She sees the display of happiness and smiles a smile I'm almost certain isn't drawn on. She raises her hand to give a thumbs-up and pins the back of her arm against her forehead in a pose of relief. Then she turns and exits in typical dramatic Miss Numero Uno fashion.

It's like the windows in the cafeteria have gotten bigger, the sky outside brighter. And when the hugging is done and I've texted Dad back, the carrots are more orange, the hemp milk is sweeter, the peanut butter tastes like it did in kindergarten.

Then I go back to the bathroom and sit in the stall and cry. *Thank you.* I say it over and over, to the merciful universe and anyone else who may be listening. *Thank you.*

17

THE WEEK FOLLOWING Echo's surgery feels strange. I didn't know how worried I was until the surgery was upon us, and then when it was over I *really* understood how worried I was.

It took a few days for Echo to adjust to her obturator, which is like a blue retainer with four fake teeth attached, to replace the four front teeth on top that were lost in the surgery. She loves taking it out and showing it to people, and when she does she looks pretty much like a first-grade kid whose baby teeth have fallen out. When she puts it back in she looks like a first-grade kid whose new teeth have grown in.

Her hair is coming in, and so is mine, like the five-o'clock shadow Dad gets on his beard at the end of the day. Or maybe even longer, like peach fuzz. I love running my hand over both our heads, and Echo loves it, too.

Thursday, I'm at the doctor with Mom and Echo. I talked my way into missing school to come along. Mom, in a celebratory mood, said yes.

I'm sitting beside Echo in the brightly lit room on the little bed that's too high and not long enough and covered with butcher-block paper. Mom sits across on a chair. There's a quick rap of knuckles on the door, and Dr. Sananda comes in. She's the one who did the surgery.

"Hello, Echo! How are you feeling today?"

"Good." Echo adores Dr. Sananda, and Dr. Sananda adores Echo. But Echo plays it cool.

"So," the doctor says, turning to Mom, "the margins look great. No malignancy in any of the test spots, and we did a dozen. And really we didn't expect to see anything. Blood looks good. So we'll give her immune system another week to bounce back, give her more time to recover from the surgery, then start the second twelve weeks of chemo next week."

"Are you kidding?" It just comes out of my mouth. "Twelve more weeks of chemo? I thought you said everything looks good!"

"Ugh!" Echo groans.

Mom looks to me. "They do it to make sure there

isn't any microscopic cancer." She turns to the doctor. "Right?"

Dr. Sananda nods. "That's correct. Everything looks very promising, but this is the protocol that's produced the best outcomes."

"We knew this was what we'd be doing," Mom says, looking at me. "But remember, we've been trying not to look too far ahead."

Echo smiles at Dr. Sananda. "Can I have my lollipop now?"

Outside the clinic, we walk in silence.

Twelve more weeks of chemo. I'm so mad I want to scream.

But I have to stay positive. I have to take my cue from Echo. And if Echo is down, I have to lift her up. *All for one, all four one.*

I'm so sick of that slogan. But it's saved us again and again.

We come to a stoplight.

Taxis and town cars whiz by.

"Mom?" I ask.

She looks across Echo to me.

"Can we take Echo someplace fun?"

She gives me a quizzical look. "What do you mean?"

"The school day is shot. By the time I get back it'll be ending."

She looks at her watch, then off into the distance, down the busy street. "I've got a dress I have to finish. I'm sorry." She looks like she'll cry.

"Don't be sorry," I say. "Thank you for working so hard for all of us. This has been tough, but you've been tougher."

She puts her hand to her heart. "Thank you for saying that."

"And I've been tough, too," I say. "I've grown a lot. So, maybe you'd let me take Echo myself?"

Mom looks to Echo, then back to me. Then back to Echo, who grins. It's the best sales pitch ever. Mom sighs, then corrects herself and tries to smile.

"Yes, you have grown." She takes the bag off her shoulder—the bag with the masks and the disinfectant wipes and the disinfectant foam and the disinfectant gel—and hands it to me. "There's money in the side pocket."

"Thank you."

"You're twelve," she says.

"Yep."

"You can handle this."

"Yes."

"Don't go far. Don't be late."

"Okay."

"I trust you."

"Thank you."

"I trust you."

"You said that."

"Hold Echo's hand."

"I will."

"Don't let go of it."

"I won't."

She bends down to kiss Echo's forehead, then mine.

"Be safe."

"We will."

"Sanitize."

"We will."

She takes a deep breath, exhales, smiles, and turns away.

I turn to Echo and smile, even though I feel like murdering the stars. I feel like murdering the universe for doing this to her.

But I *love* my sister.

Standing on the corner, the city surrounds us. It's big, and tall, and fast, and noisy. It's scary, and full of so much love I can't even get my head around it.

Twelve more weeks.

I hold Echo's hand as we walk up the block. I flag

a taxi, which I've gotten good at 'cause Dad lets me practice when we need one. I give the driver directions quietly to keep our destination a secret.

We ride up Central Park West to Sixty-Fifth and then across the park. The taxi lets us off right in front of the carousel.

"We're gonna ride the merry-go-round?" Echo asks.

"Yes!"

Her excitement kills me. She's just so happy to be here.

She pulls my arm all the way to the ticket booth. I figure I'll get her an all-day wristband if they have such a thing. That way she can ride over and over again, and she'll have a wristband that isn't from the emergency room or the hospital or the clinic for a change. 'Cause she's a six-year-old girl, and all-day-ride wristbands are the kind of wristbands six-year-old girls should be wearing. They're the kind of wristbands we *all* should be wearing.

It's a beautiful, mild day for early December, so the carousel is open. But there aren't many people here, 'cause it's the middle of a school day.

"Do you have a wristband to ride all day?" I ask.

The guy in the ticket booth shakes his head. "Nah, it's two-fifty a ride."

I look at the cash in my hand. "Can I just give you

a lot so my sister can ride it as much as she wants?"

"Aren't you gonna ride with me?" Echo asks.

"I'm not feeling well," I answer. And it's true. I feel crummy. Like I'm gonna throw up. And I feel depressed. But I smile anyway. "I wanna watch you."

The guy in the booth looks at Echo, her bald head and hopeful expression. I've got the same bald head, which I've been shaving every few days so I don't get ahead of Echo, but I no longer think about how people are looking at it. Hardly ever. The guy in the booth smiles and gives a wave of unconcern. "Ah, go ahead," he says. "My boss is a jerk."

Echo squeals and jumps up and down.

"Thank you," I say.

"Thank you!" Echo shouts.

I follow her in and wipe the carousel pony with disinfectant. I wipe the pole that runs through it. I disinfect everything in reach, using three wipes.

Then I go outside the enclosure and sit on the bench. The calliope music starts up, the carousel turns, the painted ponies go up and down.

I sit on the bench and watch Echo. She grins. She shouts "Yee-haw, giddyup!" just like I taught her years ago. She takes her hands off the shiny silver pole and waves to me. I'm thinking she might fall off, but I wave back.

It comes around again and she makes a crazy face. Her sweet little bald head sets off her big, beautiful eyes.

Each time around she waves at me. In this moment I've accidentally allowed myself to stray into thinking the cancer might return, that it might still be in her, hiding. But I wave back.

Clouds have appeared suddenly, and a raindrop falls on *my* bald head. Then another. Big thunking drops.

The rain feels different with a shaved head, like tapping a melon to see if it's ripe.

I sit in the rain and watch Echo go round and round. In my mind, each time around the carousel is another trip around the sun. Another year of life granted to Echo by the universe, which may not always be perfectly just, but which maybe sometimes can be tilted by the smallest measure.

Words play in my head to the tune of the calliope music.

Don't stop, another turn, come around again.

Don't stop, another turn, come around again.

Then the rain begins to *really* come down. People everywhere run for cover, but I stay on the bench getting soaked, watching the little kids stay dry under the shelter of the carousel.

Don't stop, another year, come around again.

I reach into the bag for one of the red Team Echo hats.

It's not the absolute worst hat I've ever seen.

I pull it on and blow a kiss to Echo as she comes around again.

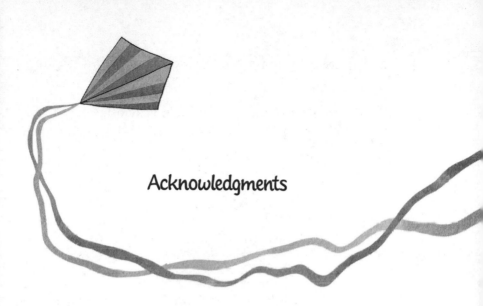

Acknowledgments

Thanks—

As always, to the mighty Central Phoenix Writer's Workshop.

In particular, Michelle Beaver and Anne Heintz, for their careful reading and helpful suggestions.

If one must experience cancer, I recommend the Coronado Historic District, the professionals at Phoenix Children's Hospital, and the concentric circles of love and humanity in the community my family has found itself the center of.

To the best literary agent, Wendy Schmalz, for believing in my work, and for adopting me into the loveliest family of writers.

To my talented editor, Karen Chaplin, and editorial director, Rosemary Brosnan, for being supportive of a troubled novelist and a book which was very difficult to give birth to.

To the muse, for not giving me a year off.

Thank you.